TAAPOATEGL & PALLET

TAAPOATEGL & PALLET

A MI'KMAQ JOURNEY OF LOSS & SURVIVAL

A NOVEL BY

PETER J. CLAIR

CHAPEL STREET EDITIONS
WOODSTOCK, NEW BRUNSWICK

Published by
Chapel Street Editions
150 Chapel Street
Woodstock, NB E7M 1H4

www.chapelstreeteditions.com

Library and Archives Canada Cataloguing in Publication

Clair, Peter J., author
    Taapoategl & Pallet : a Mi'kmaq journey of loss & survival
/ a novel by Peter Clair.

ISBN 978-1-988299-11-2 (softcover)

I. Title.

PS8605.L34T33 2017   C813'.6   C2017-905670-0

The Mi'kmaq graphic symbols on page 215 were prepared by the author and included with his permission.

The text is set in Adobe Caslon. The titles are set in Geometos Rounded.

Book design by Brendan Helmuth

DEDICATION

To Shirley and Ramona
Oelaaliôg

To those who make the world better for all
You are not alone

CONTENTS

PREFACE

This novel is a work of imagination that draws on themes and circumstances of Nigmag history and cultural survival. Any resemblance between its characters and actual persons living or dead is purely coincidental. "Nigmag," which is used throughout the book, is an old form of the name, Mi'kmaq, and describes a close kinship relationship. At the time of European colonization, the Nigmag homeland included what is now Nova Scotia, eastern and northern New Brunswick, Prince Edward Island, and part of Quebec.

Some of the characters that appear in this book are traditional figures in Wabanaki and Nigmag story telling. All depictions of these figures and the narratives of their behaviour have been created by the author.

Stories recounted by characters in the book have been drawn from narratives preserved in Nigmag oral storytelling. In one case, a character and his story – Piampit – has been created in order to depict a type of cross-cultural relationship that occurred during European colonization of the Nigmag homeland.

Nigmag words appear untranslated where the meaning is clear from the context. In cases where the meaning of the word or phrase is not clear, the translation is given in brackets when the word is used for the first time. A Glossary of Nigmag words has been provided for easy reference. Taapoategl is pronounced Tah-p-ooah-ta-kl.

Peter J. Clair
Tobique, New Brunswick

ACKNOWLEDGEMENTS

We get to where we want to be with the assistance, directly and indirectly, of many people. With gratitude and appreciation, I acknowledge the many reciprocal relationships that have helped me on my way.

I acknowledge the path of the ancestors, the land we share with all creation, and the generosity and compassion of First Nation People.

Oelaaliôg. Thank you all.

CHAPTER 1

Taapoategl's heavy sleepy eyes open in Tlaagati, a place of belonging. She closes and opens them again; the remnants of sleep fall away. She gathers her scattered thoughts that have been wandering to many summer places during the night. She often dreams about summer in the winter. In the close circular oigoôm [wigwam], she catches a whiff of her sleeping family. The familiar smell fills her with happiness and a feeling of security.

Without thinking, she dresses, passes through the blanket partition separating men and women, steps over sleeping feet, and grabs her coat hanging on a Nigmag hook. The hook began its life as a young limber maple sapling, proud and vigorous. It had aged, the shaft now split and broken, but still proud because it had been used in several ice game tournaments and has been handed down in her family. Out of habit, she touches the hook for good luck. She wishes for all to go well. Before going outside, she looks at the small, dried spruce branch, the length of an adult hand, attached to the wall. The branch is straight up and not drooping; that means no rain today.

There are large pieces of masgoi [birchbark] on either side of the oigoôm door. They have been there as long as she can remember. One piece depicts Nigmag settlements, the colours faded but the designs still clear. The piece has numerous Nigmag double curves in its design. On the other side is a masgoi piece with writing that tells the creation story of the Nigmag. This piece is often brought to gatherings and read to the community members.

Near a sitting area close to the door is a pile of masgoi that someone was probably reading last night and just left them there. There are about ten sheets with writings about past Nigmag gatherings. One sheet has a list of Nigmag who had stood together and became a couple; another has a list of babies born this year – not an exciting

1

read but interesting for someone who is looking for information about what had happened. There is one masgoi that Taapoategl especially enjoys; it tells the story of a hummingbird that would not leave the Nigmag, and which had to be kept through the winter months so it wouldn't freeze. Soon the bird learned to speak Nigmag and began to share stories about her travels and family. Taapoategl liked reading and hearing the story. Her mother has read it to her several times.

Taapoategl glances at the doorway. Hanging over the entrance are several willow sticks tied together. They are so old that bits have fallen off. She once thought it was an old broom but had been told it is her grandfather's switch. When he was a child, he did not listen to his parents. He was told he had to learn a lesson. He was told to go to the woods and gather his own switch. With tears in his eyes, he carefully gathered the softest willow he could find. He cried all the way to the place where the willow bushes grew and all the way back to the oigoôm. He gave the switch to his parents who hung it on the wall, and there it stayed as a reminder. From then on, Taapoategl's grandfather always listened to his parents. She is glad she never had to get her own switch.

Half asleep and half awake, she goes outside to feel the cold and the fullness of the world. Taapoategl enjoys rising early and is eager to greet each new day. Her father has told her that a long life comes from rising early in the morning. She steps outside the winter oigoôm, made of birchbark and furs, and walks to the fire pit in the middle of their Tlaagati. The overnight fire has burned to embers but still radiates heat. It feels good to be here. She knows she belongs-to, like many other Nigmag who also belong-to. For the old Nigmag, Tlaagati means land of belonging-to.

She picks up her water container made from birchbark and spruce roots and sealed with pitch. Her mother, Oasteo, had made it for her several years ago. It has been repaired but is still good for carrying and holding water. Taapoategl enjoys using it. She doesn't want a new one. Fetching water gives her a responsibility, a way to contribute to the family. She walks past the fire pit and on to the brook a short distance away. She thinks about how Nigmag usually

2

settle a short distance from good water. This location had been chosen in consultation with the elders who were always concerned to keep the water clean and moving.

The path to the brook, still slippery in spots, is wide enough for two people to walk side by side. Its width makes it comfortable to carry water without brushing against the tree branches. The narrow brook is flowing rapidly, clean and cold, feeding like an umbilical cord directly from the spruce and snow covered mountain.

Taapoategl kneels on the cold ground, lowering herself, stretching her arms like wings. She extends her neck to drink straight from the brook. She smells the frozen ground, the ice, the water; it all smells alive. She inhales a breath, and the water, defying gravity, rushes into her mouth, upwards in her throat, and down to her stomach.

"Tegpaag," she says, "that's cold."

She plunges her face into the water and quickly withdraws. She rubs her palms fast against her face before ice forms on her chin. It's a habit to wash her face in cold water; her relatives believe that cold water keeps the face healthy. She follows the ways of her ancestors without question.

"What fed the Nigmag feeds me too." She likes to repeat what she hears. This is what she heard from the elders. After all, she is Nigmag, from Oapenaagi, and this is her land of belonging-to, her Tlaagati.

In a graceful motion, like an eagle swooping down on a salmon, she swings her masgoi container into the brook and fills it with water. Quickly, she turns and heads back up the path, playfully moving her feet in a little dance motion and humming a song she heard last summer at the gathering. She enjoys the feeling of helping out and belonging-to. Like her, the birds, fish, plants, and animals all belong to Tlaagati.

Instead of entering the oigoôm, Taapoategl stops near the seesipeteg [fire pit] and sits on a large stone half the size of a family goiten [canoe] to feel its heat. She admires the large seesipeteg in which the fire burns all day and most of the night, and where her family gathers to cook food, keep warm, and have conversations. She thinks about how the wall of stones that circle the fire take in the heat all day and, during the cold winter months, are placed in the oigoôms at night to keep her family warm.

She thinks what a wonderful thing the seesipeteg is and how, even on cold winter evenings, some Nigmag sit outside their oigoôm on the warm stones, share food, drink tea, and tell stories about ancient relatives, or just talk about the events of the day. She shivers a bit, remembering an exaggerated tale about when it was so cold that your face would instantly freeze when crossing a frozen river or lake or an open field unless you had a masgoi mask for protection. She likes it when one of the star-readers, with a knowing and convincing glint in his eye, looks up into the clear night sky and forecasts warmer weather coming soon. There is no shortage of warm-stone stories to be heard around the fire pit.

As Taapoategl warms herself on the big stone near the fire pit, she remembers that people say the water she fetches is the best. They say her water – the first water of the day – is the freshest. She enjoys fetching water with her masgoi container and she enjoys hearing this compliment.

Sitting on the warm stone, Taapoategl remembers that during the late spring when her family was gathering birchbark, she had played among the large fallen trees, either as a squirrel running along the branches or as a quiet porcupine sitting like a knot on a tree. In the porcupine pose, she had watched her mother peel the bark from the birch tree. At this early stage of her life, it is good to learn, but on that day she was still free to play. Taapoategl remembers helping to carry pieces of birchbark back to their oigoôm where they made a water container. Her mother told her to inscribe her name on the container so it would be easy to identify if misplaced. Taapoategl inscribed two circles close to each other, each circle representing her bright eyes. Her name means "two together shining lights."

She remembers once, when the sun reached its highest peak on the longest day of the year, her mother asked her to get cold water for the grandparents. Taapoategl had jumped up, momentarily balancing on her feet, and then ran to the brook. She filled her masgoi container and ran back. She had first offered the water to her grandparents and then waited until everyone had their drink before she took a long drink. Her folks had been surprised that she was so thirsty. They asked her if she had taken a drink when she was at the brook; she had said, "No." Some family members had made eye contact and smiled.

As Taapoategl lingers, enjoying the heat of the big stone, she becomes aware that it is now the edge time between winter and spring; the time when spring takes a stand but then winter sometimes marches back, not ready to leave. The long winter has given many cold days and this was one of them. She notices the warmth of the fire pit is growing weaker, and her breath makes puffs of steam in the frigid air – a frosty reminder of her fragile existence. In her imagination, the frost patches covering the ground look like stemless mushrooms and the remaining patches of snow like large islands.

Taapoategl thinks about her life and how it will soon change as she enters her first stage of the woman's ceremony. She realizes that for the Nigmag there is always change. Even if the cold steam still rises from the brook in this edge time as it always has, she knows changes are coming. A big change had already come when the rampaging colonizers displaced the Nigmag from their homeland just when the fertile earth was becoming most bountiful.

As the morning light becomes stronger, Taapoategl thinks back over this recent change. To avoid the colonial advance and for safety and survival, some Nigmag have moved further into the woods, closer to the ancient burial grounds. Other Nigmag families have moved into the ancestral burial sites. These sites, once for ceremony, are now being used to protect the living. Some families have moved to Oôo, an old Nigmag settlement, which has a large wooden cooking pot. The pot has been there for so long no one could recall how old it was. The Nigmag have long used this settlement as a meeting place, a place to cook and share food.

Taapoategl thinks about when her family had moved to the base of Tjigon, a fertile ground that preserves the connection between

Nigmag and ancestral spirits. Her family feels safe here at the base of this mountain area on the north side of Gespiag in the northern Nigmag district. They live between two burial grounds. There is comfort here but fear as well, fear that the colonizers – the gentanteget – will come this far. But Ntjigon, like other Nigmag burial grounds, is hard to find.

Taapoategl thinks about how the grounds are hidden from the marauding thieves who steal from the Nigmag gravesites. Like the missionaries, the thieves have begun to attend Nigmag burials and know of the generosity shown towards the dead. Many Nigmag gravesites contain cultural items required to survive in the shadow-world and the next world. These items are the treasure trove the thieves are looking for. Despite the thieves and despite the missionaries telling them the practice is unnecessary, the cultural offerings at Nigmag burial ceremonies have continued. The ceremonies are now well hidden from the thieves and the missionaries probing eyes.

Taapoategl returns suddenly from her thoughts with a shudder. Her family has begun to stir. She stands up and greets each one as they emerge from their oigoôms. The fire-keepers get the fire going and a meal is prepared. After the morning meal, Taapoategl gets ready to spend the rest of the day helping her family check their trap line.

CHAPTER 2

With his eyes shut tight, Pallet smiles inside his lips. He clenches his teeth; the ones in back hurt. He knows he should have been more careful, but here he is. Despite the facial effort, a laugh sneaks up and escapes silently through his nose. It's there for all to see, but no one notices or at least comments. His eyes open and his face finally relaxes. It's a struggle, but he manages to remain composed.

As he breathes deeply, he says to himself, "Can't laugh now... can't laugh. Mndoo forbids that I laugh at my relatives. Mndoo, the Nigmag creator, would not be happy."

He must not laugh, at least, not openly at the Nigmag who are praying in unison for the two-legged ones, the four-legged ones, the winged ones, and, of course, he thinks to himself, "Let's not forget the long-winded ones."

The shaman leading the prayer continues; "May the creator bring a bountiful harvest, good health, and well wishes to all. May the diet of the good have a plump future and know no bare cupboards. May the diet of evil be quickly filled. Let compassion know no hungry ones."

Pallet listens to the shaman explain the balance of the world. There is a transparent line between evil and compassion. One is necessary like the other, necessary to survive. The fulcrum is not always in the center but often in the playground of evil.

The shaman continues his prayer, and as if to make a grandiose remark, he says, "Evil for good is no good at all."

In a dramatic concluding gesture he lowers his eyes and his head follows, like a blind follower lost in his mind. Pallet admires the shaman. When he is concentrated on a subject he doesn't diverge from it. He stays on topic; he is obsessive.

"Those Nigmag praying for the balance of evil and good," Pallet thinks, "what the hell is that?"

"Fill the evil: fill the good!" Pallet recites the shaman's prayer word for word. "As all good is not good, so all evil is not evil."

He sits quietly pondering the prayer in his mind. Balance is difficult to understand when you are living in the centre of colonial chaos.

"Praying for evil to have its fill? It's just like the Nigmag to remember the balance between evil and good in people," Pallet muses as if he understands; but it's more an acceptance of how his ancestors were, or a version of how they are now, than a full understanding.

Pallet speaks and writes the Nigmag language, but like most people he grew up with, he has difficulty fully understanding the cultural grammar. By current standards, he is considered a fluent speaker, but he feels otherwise because he knows there is so much more to learn.

"Fluency comes when you are wrapped in birchbark and become maggot food," he muses ironically. He knows he will still be learning until the end.

Pallet recalls the shaman's didactic words: "Remember, the creator loves your enemies just as much as you."

Still confused and mildly rejecting the shaman's prayer, he goes back to his anapiigan [leanto] for the night.

It has been a busy time at the gathering and he now realizes he hasn't had a Nigmag wash for a few days. Before turning in, he goes back outside to wash and cool his feet by walking through the grass, now wet with the evening dew.

As he leans on his epogan [walking stick], he swings first one foot and then the other back and forth like a metal detector looking for gold. He bends low, passing his face over the tall dew covered grass like a bumblebee gathering nectar from the night. He lies on the ground and thinks about tomorrow.

After all these years, he has finally made it to the gathering. He had no idea so many people knew he was out there travelling widely and living a solitary existence. People now want to know what he has been doing; they want to hear his story. It's been a long time since he told a story at a gathering, but he feels good and is ready to go. He is still waiting to hear from the elders about the information he presented to them. If they agree on the interpretation of the information and feel the time is right, he will speak to the gathering about the Nigmag story he has discovered.

CHAPTER 3

The story of how Pallet came to spend five years travelling and living in a solitary way begins when he was a child in Tooaatjeg, the place he was born. When quite young, he lost his parents in a whaling expedition. His family loved eating pootep [whale] and would join the harvest as often as they could. While chasing a large whale, his parents' canoe and the whale got tangled in the harpoon rope. As the whale struggled and splashed, its tail smashed their canoe. They were knocked unconscious and sank helplessly into the ocean. The other whalers were not able to rescue them. Like many Nigmag before them, his parents went to a watery grave in the ocean that provided them with an abundance of food.

Pallet has a special memory of his mother that is triggered in an unusual way. Once when he was sitting close to her as they travelled to visit her parents, she passed gas and he never forgot the smell. Many times in later life when he passed gas, it smelled like his mother and the memory of her warm comforting body came back to him.

Pallet did not want to go on that trip but it was not his choice. Once there, his grandmother greeted him and spoke to him in a low voice that made him feel better. She gave him a sweet cake, which he took under the table to eat. He heard the footsteps of a man coming who his mother greeted as "Father." Pallet did not entirely understand what was said, but he could make out that they were talking about him and how he didn't want to come and visit. His grandfather leaned down and handed him two metal disks. Pallet took the strange objects but didn't know what they were. His mother spoke and said that for someone whom did not want come and visit, he was sure paid well. Sometimes now when he passes gas, this whole happy memory flies through his mind.

After his great loss, Pallet went to live with his grandparents, Agem and Siigon. At this point in their lives, it was a reciprocal relationship and an ideal fit. The grandparents welcomed him into their home. Pallet helped with the work around their one story, two room house. His grandparents had a bedroom, while Pallet had a bed in the sitting area of the kitchen. Many an evening the grandparents shared stories of the Nigmag. They told stories of generous Nigmag and nasty Nigmag. The good and bad mingle and are mixed within one place. They seemed to add up and balance each other out. The grandparents never grew tired of telling the stories. They often retold them to stress the importance of an event. They believed that history was not to be feared, but something that steered the Nigmag to a brighter future.

His grandparents' life was one of symmetrical seasons. There was a balance in what his grandparents did; their lifeline didn't fluctuate much. The family looked forward to performing duties, sharing meals and stories. Their lives resembled the high tide line, a flat line that stretched as far as one could see. It was a natural flat line that meant all was in balance.

In the summer, his grandparents and other family members gathered in the fields to pick berries. Pallet particularly enjoyed the sand berries. They had a small white flower that turned into a white berry and eventually into a sweet red berry with small specks that looked like sand. They crushed the berries and spread them out to dry. They were then called chewberries. Chewberries were Pallet's favourite food in the winter. He'd put off eating them in the summer and fall, so he'd have some for the winter. Summer tasted best in the winter.

As pleasant as it was to pick berries in summer, there was some risk in the adventure. The family rarely brought young children along to pick berries. Grandmother Siigom always cautioned about young babies and snakes. She believed that the scent of a mother's milk in a baby's breath would attract snakes. They had to be vigilant when picking berries in the tall grass. The snake has poor eyesight so it stands straight up with head swaying in the summer breeze like the tallest timothy grass, and with its forked tongue flicking in and out trys to find a baby's breath.

Grandmother Siigon once told a harrowing tale about a snake actually crawling into a baby's mouth. Its head had disappeared inside the baby before an alert picker grabbed the snake by the throat and pulled it out. Incidents like this made some people fearful, but Pallet didn't mind snakes; he saw them as part of creation. But he respected his grandmother and accepted the story as she told it.

The boys sometimes organized snake hunting expeditions. The younger ones were convinced it was a right of passage into manhood. But, in truth, some of the older boys were dreadfully afraid of snakes. They brought the younger boys along to kill the snakes. Before the hunt, instructions were given. When the expedition got to the field, a row of the older boys would walk in unison, making noise and hitting the ground, while the younger boys waited at the other end. Unfortunately for the snakes, if there were any in the field, the younger boys had been instructed to grab their tails and snap them like a whip.

Life with grandparents was an endless source of information. They taught Pallet how to hunt for food, garden, fish, and communicate. It is easy to talk to yourself, but understanding how to talk to other people is even more important. They taught him how to read the ancient Nigmag writing. These lessons were conducted with a sheet of masgoi in a mirror-like fashion. A sheet was made into two sections, each section containing the same lesson. The teacher and student sat opposite each other and read the same text. Pallet was eager to learn the writing and reading, so it came quickly to him. He was eager to create new words, but he was careful to not overstep his bounds with his grandparents. He respected the knowledge in their blood and realized he was becoming a part of it.

His grandparents told many stories. Some of the stories were about young relatives who went travelling. The Nigmag would travel at various stages of their lives. Some left as adults but some left much earlier. Some left even before their first moon ceremony and before they were able to contribute fully to the community. Some left for many years and then returned as adults, and sometimes even with new families. Some travellers did not return and were never heard from again.

Pallet had heard the stories so often he could recite them from memory. Learning from what he heard, he made sure that he was contributing to the community. He would sometimes fish all night and leave what he caught by the road for others to take home.

The stories left a deep impression on him. He knew it was important to learn and tell stories. His grandparents knew stories had to be shared again and again so their lessons, both old and new, would be learned and fully appreciated. In addition to the stories told in the evening, the grandparents would repeat the stories whenever they had company or at gatherings. Often times, their company had heard the stories before, but they were still fascinated to hear them again. Sometimes when there were many visitors, the guests were divided into groups and Pallet would tell one story to one group while the grandparents spoke to another group. No one asked any questions. They just listened and were always willing to hear the stories over and over again. Pallet came to understand all these stories as a kind of cultural saga, a kind of poetic chronicle of the Nigmag that carried lessons and wisdom to be shared.

From an early age Pallet wanted to travel and explore Tlaagati. And, if the opportunity arose, he would travel beyond his homeland and explore the homeland of the neighouring Sgiitjin, the above-ground dwellers. He would acknowledge the above-ground dwellers territory, seek permission to enter, and offer gifts to his hosts.

Even though he was happy where he was, surrounded by family and a secure healthy environment, he still wanted to travel. It did not matter if he met people or not in his travels, or where his travels took him, he was ready to leave. As a young man, he felt he had heard it all, now he wanted to see it all. He wanted to explore and felt confident that people would still take care of each other after he left. He knew many people who would stay. They would tend to the living, bury the dead, and feed the young even though they were no longer connected to the ancient Nigmag philosophy. But despite this longing to travel and explore, he stayed put because he felt he had family obligations. He wanted to care for his grandparents who were so generous with him. The choice to stay was made easier by his love for his grandparents.

Then, in his late teens, Pallet's world completely changed in a short time. He came home one evening as people were gathering at his grandparents' house. He thought it must be people who wanted to hear his grandparents' stories. But as he came closer, he saw grandfather come out and yell, "Come tonight and share our feelings. Our aunt has left us." Pallet hurried to his grandfather. They hugged each other.

"It's alright. We will be fine," his grandfather said. They both cried tears they didn't know they had.

In the spring, his grandmother took her last breath. She had often mentioned that after her last breath, she was eager to take her first breath in the other world. For Pallet there were many things to remember her by, but one he especially recalled was the time she told him; "You are Nigmag. Now find out who you are." Pallet was perplexed by the advice, but even more so when she said; "It can be hard to be happy when you don't know who you are."

It was a sad time for grandfather. He didn't want to eat or participate in the funeral. Many people came with gifts and condolences. The burial singers came and sang all night. This was to ensure Siigon was not lonely on her journey and that she would arrive safely. Despite his sadness, grandfather remembered to pass many sheets of masgoi to Pallet.

"Here," he said, "Your grandmother wanted you to have these. Take them."

His grandparents had strong ties and only death could break the ties of these life long partners. After her body was wrapped in masgoi, grandfather continued to sit nearby. He said she would not leave him for long. He wanted to go and be with her. His prophecy came true and he passed on before the moon was done. As in their life, she broke the path to deal with many choices and roads to take, and now she led the way into the other world and he was not far behind. Both burials were elaborate. Pallet had many preparations to make. He also had to acknowledge the people who had travelled great distances to offer support for the family. Family members had to be supported and grief had to be acknowledged.

It was late fall before he felt right about the opportunity to leave. At first, he did not want to leave. There were still family members who were grieving and it would be a cold time of year to travel. But hot or cold, it did not matter. He had grown up to deal with environmental situations as they came. The season should not matter as long as he was well prepared and enjoyed it. Neither season nor reason could stop his wanderlust. He had been ready to go for a long time. He was confident he could care for himself in any circumstance. He had taken good care of his family and had been responsible to his community. Now, he had to travel and explore. Pallet remembered his grandfather saying, "Be careful where you are and where you want to be. In retrospect, it's one place."

He had lost his parents and grandparents; it was now time to go. For now he must leave home behind and find places that are not home. But, at the same time, he knew that home is always between the eyes.

A hard winter moon overhead had passed when he first set up his camp near a stream that emptied into a large lake. The lake would have plenty of fish. Here he rested, thought about what he wanted to do and made plans to travel further when summer returned. Living alone, he set about to implement all the survival skills he had learned from his family.

* * * * *

For first year Pallet was mostly alone, living in the deep woods and travelling widely. During this time he steadily improved his survival skills and matured from a hidden loneliness. He avoided Nigmag gatherings and the moccasin path. He stayed away from roads. Occasionally, he passed near a settlement or a cabin occupied by hunters or fisherman. He kept the contacts brief and moved on. From these few contacts, however, conversations about Pallet spread in Tlaagati and Sgiitjin. During the second year he remained entirely to himself avoiding all contact with others. His solitary existence was by choice, which over time gave him a feeling of great self-reliance. Spruce trees and stones were not great company but, for now, he did not feel the need to be around other people.

Pallet carried his belongings in a leather bag made from moose hide and an ash splint backpack loaded with supplies, tools, and extra clothes. The bag had a wide shoulder strap. The front of the bag was decorated with icons that celebrated Nigmag life and history. The decorations on the bag served as a record of what had to be preserved so that each new generation would remember.

The leather bag was often saturated on the outside with early morning dew when he was bushwhacking through an area with no trails. It was sometimes well drenched when a sudden rainstorm caught him with no shelter at hand. The wet bag then had its own peculiar odour. It smelled of wet moose, dried sweetgrass, and his nuts and berries harvest. The bag was a constant reminder that the lives of animals and plants must be taken so the Nigmag can live. The waterproof bag kept a change of clothes dry, his maps legible, and his head clear.

Pallet could not recall where or when he had gotten the bag; he wanted to think his mother left it by his side when he was a child. He had been using the bag for such a long time, and from such a young age, that his shoulder had a slope matching the limp of his left leg, a reminder of an injury in his younger days. Despite the slight physical deformation from carrying it, Pallet loved his bag. It was part of his identity. Bags like this always seemed to carry secrets. They have the feeling of history and history has secrets. Pallet did not feel he had any secrets but the bag gave him the appearance of someone who had many secrets and he enjoyed the distinction. He would have gladly shared secrets if he knew what they were.

His cultural appearance and continuous travel gave him an aura of unusual experience and an air of mystery, which he did not discourage. Basically, he just lived from day to day, enjoying life as it was dished out to him. He didn't care if it rained or if the sun shone, he was always willing to accept the necessities of natural forces and events.

Pallet was deeply interested in history but sometimes found it hard to understand history because we all breathe the same air as those who have passed on. The age of cultural awareness or, some would say, the age of regret, had crept up on him. He remembered events he would now handle differently. His bag was also decorated with designs that resonate with mysterious meanings, like the double curves pointing outward, a sign of entry. He was ambivalent about the designs because he felt some traditions served as a cultural umbilical cord that tied him to responsibilities he must fulfill. He had promised his grandmother he would share Nigmag history with the next generation who were continuously arriving. There seemed no end to the new generation's appetite to arrive. This is the way the world is; the last to arrive is also always the first.

Perhaps it was a good thing that Pallet was mostly alone the first two years after his grandparents' death. The loss of his family left him wondering what to do, and the burden stayed silently with him. During this time, he rethought his memories of home over and over. After many sessions of memory visitation, he knew he would not be able to return home. Home is where you are, not where you were. Where you were is not where you are. You are always where you have to be.

Without realizing it, however, Pallet had now been alone too long. The longer he was alone the more his self-conversations, although colourful and thoughtful, were increasingly one-sided. Living alone, he began to see a perfect world and whatever he did as having a meaningful purpose. If he came across a fallen tree, he would perform a ceremony for it, speaking in hushed tones. If he had to cut down a tree, he made every effort to plant another. When he caught a fish, he would remove debris from the stream so more fish could thrive there. It was an extreme existence. Without people around, he had no need to compromise or practice social skills.

He was trying to live in a perfect world. If people had been around him, they would have told him he was obsessive and that his standard of mutual relationships was just too high. No one could meet his standard. He would not have understood why others would not listen to his suggestions, why they didn't do things the right way. He would have been quick to give them the full treatment of his view of a perfect world.

All this was before Pallet fell in the river for the second time and nearly drowned. All this was a prelude to a change that was coming.

During the first winter he was travelling and living alone, he crossed a frozen river in a place where he had crossed before. His sense of caution was not on alert. Suddenly, the ice gave way and he was swept downstream into rough water. He tried to swim but the water was too fast and rough. He bobbed and tumbled like a cork. He at least managed to keep his head above water until he fetched up on a big tree fallen from the shore into the river. He crawled out, shook himself like a dog, and made his way back to camp. He took that one in stride.

Over a year later he was camped by another river during the spring freshet. He had made a log bridge extending from the shore of the river to a large rock. He knew that trout hung out around the tail end of the rock where he could clearly see them and catch them by hand. He was getting good at this kind of fishing. Crouching on the rock, he bent forward and scooped up a trout. He held it tightly in both hands but the trout was not ready to give up. It slipped out of his hands and landed back in the water. Pallet was not far behind as he lost his balance and slipped on the wet rock. The fast flowing water of the spring freshet made it impossible to swim with any control. He spread out his arms to catch hold of something but without success. He kept tumbling wildly downriver, taking in too much water. He became disoriented and virtually passed out. Suddenly, his jacket snagged on the limb of a fallen and partly submerged tree. He came to, grasped onto the tree, and slowly dragged himself to shore. He made it back to his campsite and stoked up the fire to dry his clothes and get warm. He was chilled to the bone. This one he did not take in stride. This time he had nearly lost his life.

CHAPTER 4

Several mornings after his near drowning, Pallet wakes up and stokes his campfire into a good hot blaze. But then, oddly, it becomes smoky. Smoke rolls out over his campsite hurting his eyes. He can hardly see anything.

"Get off your high rock, Nigmag."

Pallet is not sure what he has heard. There is no one around. He thinks it must have been the burning sensation in his eyes that is talking to him.

"You heard me. Get off your mighty rock, Nigmag."

"Who are you? Where are you?"

"Open your bloodshot eyes and you'll see."

Pallet hesitates. Is he ready to see anybody? It has been too long. He opens his eyes but all he sees is smoke.

"I can't see you, whoever you are; but I can hear you."

"Funny. Seems like you're seeing everything else."

Pallet stumbles past the fire and goes to the river to wash his eyes. He regains some vision and now sees a shadowy image. He is not sure how many there are. He squints his eyes toward his campfire; there is a dark round cloud above it.

Admitting to his confused state he says: "Ok. I'm Pallet and I'm from Signigtog. I can barely make you out. All I see is a dark cloud of smoke. I am glad you are here. I have been alone for so long. Are you from Tlaagati? Are you here to help?"

"Don't be jumping to conclusions. Don't be too hasty. Rest your eyes, Nigmag. It'll come to you. My name is Miigemooesso.

You've probably heard about me. I'm the one who helps out once in a while. I don't know why. People around here should be allowed to live their own lives. But there are bigger plans than you or me. We are but paddlers on masgoi. Let's paddle in the same direction. What do you say, Nigmag?"

"Yes, I've heard about you. I am not quite sure what you do. I think you're a whiz with oaltesg. You haven't lost a game yet."

"Show me the maple burl and bone dice, and I'll show you how to play. I can make those wafer thin dice dance through the air to the tune of my song."

"Perhaps, later." Pallet feels intimidated.

Pallet pauses and moves closer to the fire. He strains to see and then says: "It's still smoky. I know you're a bit small. Maybe that's why I can't see you."

For a brief moment, he sees a woman with braided hair and a knowing smile. Pallet knows the Miigemooesso can be mischievous, so he is careful not to incite her. He has enough to do without drawing attention to himself. He wanted to be alone to figure out what he should do with his life. He had lived the life his family had prepared for him, and he didn't know what to do when he had a chance to do whatever he wanted. But after long time of being alone, he still is not sure of what to do.

The elders had said they were many Miigemooesso in the forest, but they did not restrict the location of their activities. They moved around and you never knew when, if at all, you would be fortunate enough to see them. You could live your whole life and not see one. If you do see one, you'll go blind.

Pallet thinks, "What's the difference; I'm half blind with smoke already."

"No, I'm not small. We think of our size as fetching. But that's how we view ourselves. To you we are small. But I won't argue. Small, tall – it's all there to see."

"The elders say no one has ever seen you."

"Yeah. A few of us have gotten away from that."

"So I won't go blind!"

"At the rate you're going, you're going to be blind by your own hand, not from seeing me. I should be so lucky."

"Ouch! You've got an edge. Ouch, a sharp tongue too."

Pallet glances toward her feet, but she has moccasins on and he can't see them. Without logic or reason, he had quickly thought she might have claws on her feet.

"And there are no claws or split hoofs down there either. For an above-ground dweller, you have some weird thoughts. These are your thoughts and not your elders, I presume."

"Yes. Sorry. I should focus," says Pallet trying to act like a submissive puppy. He smiled as if he was wagging his tail.

"Well, do you remember the fallen tree in the water?"

"There are many fallen trees."

"Well, this one didn't fall on you but it was in the river when you fell through the ice. Think Nigmag. I know you're still a bit dazed with what's going on. Calm it down and think it out."

"Yes... aah... no. I'm not sure. Yes, yes, I remember. That was a close call. I should be more careful."

"Good. Ok. I'm glad you don't have to relive that one."

"I'm just trying to be honest, but I'm not used to this sort of thing. I've heard stories about people running across a frozen lake with ice that is eyebrow hair thin. There are other stories like that and I accepted the stories for what they were. I have to accept that you are here. You are not just a story anymore."

"Well, do you remember the second fallen tree in the river?"

"No... yes. Yes, I remember. That's the one when I fell into the swift moving water. I have to say that was a tremendous piece of luck. I was a goner. I don't remember much of it, just dragging myself to

23

shore. Thank goodness, I didn't have to be revived. It would have been hard trying to revive myself. A fumal enema would have been difficult to maneuver at the time. I would have had to... Well, you get the picture."

"Well, that's two already. Some would say you've had two miracles. I'm here to tell you to stop wasting your miracles. You have to loosen some seams in your masgoi a bit, and enjoy what life you have left. If you don't want these miracles, give them to someone who can use them. And don't worry if you cannot remember. It either has happened or is yet to happen. They don't always tell me. Anyway, there you are. If you didn't know before, you know now."

Pallet feels reprimanded and is still confused. He needs more time to understand or he will get further confused. He wonders where they are. Are they still at his camp or somewhere else?

To change the topic he says, "I have some venison. It's fresh and I was going have some today. You are welcome to stay and eat."

"No thanks. Just feed the fire. That's fine with me. I never know what kind of appetite I have. Last time I couldn't get enough of river pebbles – weird or what? I know it may be a bit of a stretch to believe, but I never know what or where I'll be. For now I am here, and the fire is doing wonders for my skin."

"Ok. And yes, you are a surprise for me too."

Pallet is still wondering who this person is, if she is a person. He remembers his father saying: "When in doubt, offer assistance."

"What can I do for you?"

By now Pallet sees a small woman dressed in leather, sitting on top of his campfire. She is holding a pipe similar to one his grandmother used to have, which she affectionately called her "rump pipe." (Pallet had not understood the reason for the pet name and it had not been for him to ask. "Maybe if I had fought a whale with my bare hands, I would have earned the right to ask.") He keeps his eyes pointed directly at Miigemooesso. He doesn't rub his eyes in case she may disappear if he momentarily loses sight of her.

"Occasionally, I am sent out to deliver a message. I think you got the message. You'll have to do the rest. Just remember when smoke burns your eyes, it's time to cool down. Now stoke the fire. I like the smoke."

Pallet runs to fetch wood and stokes the fire. He is glad that Miigemooesso is still there. He watches her as she rubs smoke all over herself in a way similar to his grandmother when she prayed with sweetgrass. She would burn it and wave the smoke all over herself for protection.

Pallet is glad to have company, and such unusual company she is. They do not talk much. It is as if Pallet is locked in a trance. He is mesmerized watching her bathing in the smoke and can't move. The fire begins to die down, and as quickly as he can, he goes for more wood. With a stack of wood inside his elbow, he runs and stumbles, falling on the ground spilling the wood in front of him. He is afraid to look up, hoping his company did not see him fall. When he looks up, Miigemooesso is gone.

He stands quietly, disappointed. His world is again his own. He strains to hear something familiar. Not sure, he thinks he hears his grandmother. Even if he hasn't heard his grandmother, he is glad for any thoughts of her that come to him. He feels reassured.

He returns to the fire, which has gone out. He feels the warm, dusty ashes, and finds several sheets of masgoi where Miigemooesso had been. They are not burnt or discoloured. He knows they mean something, but he's not sure what. He will keep them safe. Pallet now knows he has to leave his hermit life and get back to living with people.

While it is still daylight, he begins to gather his belongings and prepares to leave. He travels with only the necessities. He cannot begin to carry all he collected while he was living alone. Now, there is an urgency to move lightly. He begins travelling as quickly as he can.

He travels for a quarter of a moon before he reaches a cabin near a lake where Siipit, an elderly Nigmag woman, lives. Pallet has met her once in a dream, but this is more than he expected. She is agile for her years even though she has lost the front part of one foot in a canoeing accident. She doesn't care who sees her half foot. She enjoys life and is jolly quick to tell a joke.

Soon after they meet, Pallet excuses himself to go to the outhouse. Siipit affectionately offers her cupped hands and lowers her head as if to receive a sacrament. Pallet is surprised and embarrassed. She laughs and laughs at his reaction. She laughs from inside her belly.

* * * * *

Spring comes fast. It is a blessed time of the year for the two Nigmag living in the small cabin. Both Siipit and Pallet have their duties during the day. Sometimes they don't see each other all day. Some evenings, Siipit leaves the camp and returns in the morning with a basket full of fish or berries. There is always plenty of fresh food. Once Pallet has the courage to ask where the food comes from. Siipit said it was from Potlatamootj, who could be a mischievous character but also could be generous. Pallet knows about Potlatamootj. He has met Miigemooesso, so he doesn't question his host. He knows that Miigemooesso and Potlatamootj are similar.

"Sometimes," Pallet muses, "one has to accept what happens rather than understand it."

Siipit has masgoi containers, pegs, and a drill for collecting the sweet sap of the maple tree that is now starting to flow. They are both eager for the first sap run. They are looking forward to making tea sweetened with maple sap. Pallet uses the drill to bore small holes in the maple trees. He inserts the hollow pegs and hangs the masgoi containers. The sap runs quickly and soon they have plenty to sweeten their tea. They rejoice in the pleasure of sharing the maple sap tea. They collect maple sap until there is enough to boil down and make syrup. Pallet enjoys the work of making this sweet delight. It helps reconnect him to the Nigmag.

Siipit has a lot of sweetgrass. The aroma takes Pallet back to his younger days. During quiet times, the aroma of sweetgrass rekindles memories of his youth, especially of his canoe that he kept behind grandmother's house and is now probably long rotted away. He had often used the canoe to cross the river and collect sweetgrass. He would burn sweetgrass to accompany his prayers or as a serenity smudge to calm a stressful situation. The smell of the sweetgrass is a constant reminder of his Nigmag family.

Siipit has a two-room cabin, with a bedroom and a living area where everything is done: sorting medicines, cleaning game, playing a dice game called oaltesg. It is room of many activities. The house is lit with an oil lamp and with light from the fireplace. In the evening, the room is dimly lit and dark in some areas. The room has the perfect ambiance for telling stories. Siipit enjoys stories and is a great storyteller.

She remembers many events in Nigmag life, but Pallet is especially interested in stories of Nigmag who went travelling. Siipit says she remembers some of her relatives had once lived at Tjigon. They had moved there to escape the bounty hunters. She says the area had a concentration of people who used to write on masgoi to communicate. She doesn't give more details and Pallet doesn't ask. If he is bound to know then he will know.

Later, even though Pallet asks no questions, Siipit is ready to tell a story about the night people that she had heard from her uncle, Oiipit. Pallet has already heard the story from his father, but he wants to hear it again; it is always good to get another version to confirm an event. Siipit begins the story.

"Sitamog was a religious leader. He and his followers were mostly active during the night. The night worshipers were connected to an ancient story about what people did during dark periods of history when the sun would not shine through the clouds for many a full moon. This old story took on a special meaning as the new religion from Europe was beginning to uproot the Nigmag ancient beliefs and traditions. At this time, Sitamog was beginning to gather followers. Crowds gathered to see and hear him. His message was simple: first, responsibility to family, and if there is any energy left then responsibility to god. In the end, attendance to family was the foundation for the religion; family came first before god.

27

"One summer, Oiipit was travelling with other Nigmag. They made camp near a large lake where they could be seen from a great distance, a sort of beacon and an invitation to come and visit. One night, sitting by the campfire, they heard a rustling in the woods and instinctively tried to see what or who it was. Maybe it was a rabbit looking for twigs to nibble. They didn't see anyone. Then they saw human figures walking near the camp, but they didn't stop, which was unusual. Some were carrying fishing gear and baskets. Some had bows and arrows.

"Oiipit was surprised they were moving so quickly and with such ease in the dark. One of the other Nigmag, sitting with Oiipit, said they were night worshipers who performed their duties during the night. They would fish, fetch wood, hunt, and gather medicine at dawn or dusk. The night worshipers soon became prolific suppliers of food. Other Nigmag came to their evening gathering because they offered so much food to the community.

"Sitamog began to give speeches about Nigmag history he had heard from the elders. He had an uncanny skill for remembering the history of the Nigmag. Unintentionally, Sitamog speeches took on the tone of sermons. People began to talk about his stories and the food he was getting from the night.

"Rumours began to spread that Sitamog came from a long line of messenger runners who specialized in running at night. Like a rabbit, he knew all the old trails. Even trails that had been abandoned, he somehow knew where they were. It was in his blood; he knew how to move at night. People said he knew the trails so well that rabbits would follow him.

"It was not long before the night worshipers posed a threat to the new European religion that had been taken up by the Nigmag. Some Nigmag elders did not support this new night religion. They would dismiss any discussion by saying that they had not heard of such events. Despite elder opposition, the night worshipers were recreating ancient traditions and religious practices. Some of Sitamog's family did not like the burden of being related to the leader of a religious cult, and some did not believe or follow him.

Speculation set in. They became fearful when they realized the possible repercussions for the community that may arise if the new European religion was questioned or challenged. The family decided that something had to be done.

"During the midsummer moon, four family members descended on Sitamog's oigoôm and while he slept, four bloody deadly blows were delivered. The bloody deadly deed was done. Sitamog was covered totally in masgoi and given a proper Nigmag burial at high noon. Orations followed and the family spoke of how, in the end, Sitamog was regretful for questioning the new religion and for starting the night worshipers' religion. Half a moon later, the body was reburied at an unknown location. The unknown site would keep his followers from creating a sacred meeting ground. It was not long until the night worshipers disbanded and returned to their previous lives of daytime activities."

Siipit finishes her story with a "Taagô." She sips on the Labrador tea that is ever present on her stove. She loves the smell and taste of the tea. She also loves stories.

She hands Pallet a fresh cup of tea and says; "Now it's your turn for a story."

He doesn't have to be asked twice. Pallet has what people called "story memory." He can remember from tip to tail any story he has heard. It has been a long time since he has told a story.

When he lived with his grandparents, he was hearing and telling stories all the time. In this way, a lot of history was preserved. He knew that the stories of history didn't always appear in a neat masgoi package smelling of sweetgrass and spring flowers. He knew there were stories between oigoôm and castles that need to be told.

Pallet has always been willing to gather stories from people who are not always congenial and sometimes adversarial. He has an understanding of how to deal with such people. Sometimes it is best to just listen. Storytellers want to be heard and it's not always safe to interrupt them. "Do not disturb a fragile ego," is Pallet's motto.

This time he reaches for a story his grandmother told one summer evening when the fireflies were lighting up the night sky like a thousand pôgteoitn [meteors], the story about the first great baptism of the Nigmag in 1610.

"It was a difficult time. The cousins were waging war over who was going to eventually control the land of the Nigmag. That was the mantra of the cousins. But by now the Nigmag had made strides in arranging marriages with the cousins who had come from across the water. The Nigmag saw an opportunity to Nigameoeiataig the world [to spread Nigmag influence through intermarriage]. If the Nigmag and the cousins could not agree on a plan, then having children together would get the discussion moving. It would be better to share the land and the future with the people who were at least part Nigmag. But the cousins had their own plans for speeding up the process of colonization and land control, which involved using religion and the power of baptism.

"One of the more fraudulent grabs to speed up colonization was to baptize Saasap, one of the better-known district chiefs. He was a respected leader because of the equality he incorporated into his leadership and his life. For all Nigmag, life and death are born into one. They converge and life ends. When this happened to Saasap, it was late winter in the most northern section of Nigmagaagati. Word of his death quickly spread. Runners spread the news. Messages were scratched on birch trees. Volunteers offered help. Rolls of masgoi were donated to cover and protect Saasap's remains for the journey back to his birthplace where his bellybutton was buried. Nigmag buried the bellybutton where they were born. Children were always told where their bellybuttons were buried to ensure they knew of their beginnings. Some Nigmag made a yearly pilgrimage to where their bellybutton was buried. Other families were brought along to remind them of where Nigmag land had been settled. The elders said that Nigmag considered the land to be settled once they buried their bellybutton there. So there are millions of Nigmag bellybuttons buried in Tlaagati.

"Like his ancestors before him, Saasap's remains were covered in masgoi, brimming with gifts, and sewn shut. Come hell or high water, the remains would be safe in masgoi. There was nothing safer than to be buried in masgoi. The journey back to the burial ground took a half a moon, and usually the Nigmag burial would have soon followed, but Saasap had made a request to be buried in the summertime. According to his wishes, the remains were placed on a scaffold until then. Many well-wishers came to offer condolences and assistance, and to renew friendships and alliances. This ceremony was referred to as saalitei, and was a time to demonstrate generosity. Among the many visitors were the cousins who had begun to gain influence with their promise of the greatest afterlife, a real Nigmag utopia, but which no Nigmag could enjoy unless they were baptized. In this promised land, there was an abundance of venison, fish, fowl, vegetables and fruits; there was no sickness and there were no disagreements. Some of the staunch Nigmag were heard to say, 'We already have that right here.'

"Gentle, persuasive pressure was exerted on Saasap's family for the missionaries to offer a ceremony and prayers at the burial, so that he would be welcomed into the great utopia. When he arrived there, they promised, he could make preparations for the rest of his family and other Nigmag to enter the utopia also. He could prepare food, dry fish, pick berries and prepare the place for his relatives.

"After much pressure, the family agreed to the request for the priest to do the ceremony. Needless to say, when the time came for the burial, many visitors – friends and enemies – filled the shores of the bay where Saasap wanted to be buried with many of his relatives. This was not an unusual request. At the burial, many people spoke, cried, laughed, and the shaman shook his rattles. Before the masgoi, laden with gifts, medicines, and tools, was placed in the ground, the missionaries offered their ceremony.

"Without proper observance of Nigmag burial ceremony, the missionaries began what was later called a baptismal requiem. They sprinkled water on the masgoi coffin, shaking their rosary beads like a rattlesnake, and thus, according to them, baptized the heathen, which opened the gates of the great utopia. With the sprinkling of the water and shaking of the beads on Saasap, the cousins' history records their first Nigmag baptism. After the baptism, the missionaries continued to mumble incomprehensible and strange words, which they hastily ended with… 'In peace.' Later, and to their surprise, many Nigmag learned their grand chief had been baptized posthumously. The Nigmag were puzzled and didn't know what to say. They could not understand this dark satire, this baptism of the dead. Despite the unorthodox practice, the Nigmag were willing to respect the cousins' religion."

Like his grandfather, Pallet concludes the story by saying, "Not one of the Nigmag's brightest moments. Taagô."

CHAPTER 5

The night-walking moon moves through tes ag mo tes [time and no time] and towards warmer weather, but it is still cold. Taapoategl, like other Nigmag children, enjoys the winter. There is a saying in the settlement, which the children sing; "Winter be fun." Then the parents would sing; "Winter be done." Each verse was a celebration accompanied by a small dance.

Despite the cold, Taapoategl rises early. She hurries toward the brook with her masgoi container, which is just big enough to hold water for making tea. This morning, as she performs her duty, she decides to first drink from the brook. Like a deer reaching to drink water, she extends her mouth and throat downward toward the brook. Taapoategl is in an unbalanced position; she is not totally aware of her surroundings. But despite all this, she feels safe in Tlaagati; she has the secure feeling of belonging-to.

The well-hidden gentanteget watch as she drinks from the brook. They remain quiet and keep six eyes on her. The hunters watch in deadly silence. They hold their breath like one who is ready to squeeze a trigger. They do not want to alert the other Nigmag. Then, on the hillside of the brook, one of the getaanetget stands and makes a sudden noise to frighten the girl. Taapoategl sees him. She is startled, panics, turns, and runs into another one who is now standing in front of her. She loses her footing and her breath. The masgoi container flies through the air and lands in a willow bush. Before she can regain her balance, she is pushed to the ground from behind by another gentanteget who roughly covers her mouth and eyes with a piece of woolen cloth and puts a sack over her head.

"Gitjoo… Gitjoo… Gitjoo… apôenmoi… apôenmoi…," [mother, help me] she screams, but her frantic call for her mother's help dissolves into the woolen cloth. Pain muffles her voice. No one hears.

A gentanteget strikes her in the back of the head and jabs her lower back with a stick. She loses her breath and curls up. She is hurt into silence. Her right glove falls off and dangles from her sleeve as she keels over. She tries to rise by bracing herself on the ground. The frosted ground is solid under her warm palm, but she is confused... confused... out of breath, unable to rise and collapses onto the ground. She lapses into momentary unconsciousness, and only sees dark red, almost black.

Another gentanteget pounces on her and tightly secures the sack with a rope. Another strikes her in the stomach to further disorient her into a submissive state of surprise and shock. They bind her hands and feet and prop her up. She falls. They prop her again and again she falls. The gentanteget are breathing hard; their hearts are racing from their victim's capture. They are exhausted, their throats are dry, but they must move.

The cold air is now steaming with the commotion and full of frost crystal dust. The gentanteget are efficient and proceed without hesitation. They have done this before. One of them grabs Taapoategl and tosses her on his shoulder. They move swiftly through the leafless forest, careful not to leave a trail. She struggles to free herself but is struck with a stick each time she tries. They know where to strike her without causing permanent damage. She will later be valuable to them; she will bring a good price.

After some distance, the gentanteget begin to take turns carrying her. She tries to determine in which direction they are moving. She moves her hand around to feel heat from the morning sun, but there is no sun today. She listens for the river to tell which way it is flowing, but there are no sounds of the river. She smells the spruce and the needles prick her hand. This is the only thing that is familiar. They are real, but where is she?

The gentanteget rarely rest and when they do they turn her around several times so she doesn't know where she is. And when they leave they turn her around several times again. By now she knows there are three gentanteget because each time they switch off carrying her, they each smell different. By their smell she knows the

34

gentanteget are not Sgiitjinoog who are the neighbouring above-ground dwellers. The Sgiitjinoog are ancient relatives of the Nigmag. The relatives had lived apart for centuries and developed their own philosophies. Like the Nigmag, the Sgiitjinoog are careful about keeping clean. Even in the winter, they enter the sweat lodge to stay clean and renew their nourishing spiritual connection with the ancestors. She knows the gentanteget are not sweat lodge users.

Taapoategl knows it is getting dark because it is getting colder and she doesn't see any light. The wool cloth around her eyes has loosened and slipped down. Later, they stop to rest for the night and eat what meager provisions they have, but they do not build a fire. She is not fed. One of them removes her hood and gives her a sharp tap with a stick on the shoulder to remind her to keep quiet. He holds the stick over her head. He puts the hood back on her. To keep warm, they all sit close together beneath a fallen tree. Tied to another tree, she sits away from them – cold, hungry, and thirsty. She doesn't sleep much. Her stomach hurts from having been carried on their shoulders.

The morning is still dark when the gentanteget begin to stir. They remove the sack from her head and tie her hands to a tree. She relieves herself and eats snow to quench her thirst. One of them comes over and covers her eyes, mouth and head again. He pushes her to start walking; she refuses. He ties her again and leaves. Soon all the gentantegets return and force her down on the ground. They bind her hands and legs.

CHAPTER 6

Living with Siipit brings Pallet out of his solitary ways. He couldn't have asked for a better companion at this stage of his quest. She is like a grandmother, but a funny, and in some ways, strange grandmother. He knows this reconnection with people is part of the change that is coming, but only part. Some part is still hidden and he needs to find out what it is. Pallet decides to start travelling again. He packs up his essential goods, bids a fond goodbye to Siipit, and sets out on an old grass covered road that leads away from the lake into the woods.

Pallet walks like the old timers, eyes straight on. "Feel your walk. Feel the earth. You'll know where you are," he remembers them saying. After walking several days, he is not sure where he is. Lost? No... he's not lost; he's just between the place where he had been and the place he is going to.

He comes to an abandoned road with new growth closing in and parts of it washed out. He thinks it may have been a railroad bed. He had once heard of a train that transported Nigmag remains from Pitjipogeg. This may be near the place where, according to the story, railroad builders found an ancient Nigmag burial site. They dug it up and removed the Nigmag remains that were wrapped in sacred masgoi. The masgoi was cut open and spread out like a morning newspaper. The Nigmag lay naked and disrespected by the roadside. The gifts that had been included in the Nigmag burials quickly disappeared.

A thousand years of culture gone in one night. Pallet heard of the event from travelling Nigmag who knew the burial site and the story. Shots had been fired overhead by the railroad builders to keep the Nigmag at a distance. But there was enough evidence left to tell the story of what had happened.

Later, Pallet comes to a place where the road widens out. As he glances around he sees two roads at the other end of the clearing, one with a derelict gate and another with a basaltic stone in the middle. The gate is decayed from long exposure to many winter winds and the heat and rain of many summers. Broken pieces of wood are scattered on the ground around the gate. The stone is rounded from water and weathering. Many small pieces have fallen off the stone and are scattered around it on the ground.

Pallet is unsure which way to go. He thinks it would be more interesting to venture into uncertainty than into the safety of the well known. He muses momentarily about letting faith decide, but he doesn't want to go there. Faith has troubles of its own. Uncertainty is not comforting him today; he feels like travelling a beaten path. He is weary of travelling on the alder route.

He can't decide which way to go… left or right? He knows he wants to go where there are people.

"How do I decide?" Pallet says under his breath. "Is there security in indecision? Absolutely. With indecision, there are no expectations. I love indecision. I love having no expectations. Life seems fuller without expectations, but one must move to enjoy the indecision. So which way do I go, left or right?"

To the right was the derelict gate with a smoky portal behind it; to the left is the large stone, about the size of a bear.

"To the left."

With sense of instant relief, Pallet goes left. Stones have been around longer than gates. He is not sure of the direction, but he is sure of the decision.

As he enters the path, he hears a voice.

"Hold it, Aptoon. What's yus business? Shouldn't be here."

Pallet looks to the right with his good left eye and there sits a pile of a figure. The pile has a stomach that protrudes like a bruised crab apple in the fall. His hands are covered with brown pitch, like he doesn't bother cleaning them. He looks like he has enjoyed too many deer steaks or salmon tails. His jacket, torn and oily, resembles a silk tablecloth full of evidence of many meals.

"Gi'sus, you startled me."

Pallet was still getting accustomed to talking to people.

"What's yus business, Aptoon?"

Pallet wonders why he is being called a cane. "I'm returning. I'm going to the gathering. And yourself? What's your business, mister sir?"

Pallet can't resist the sarcasm; it tastes sweet, but it is not really a taste he wants to acquire.

"Here to put my eye on ye. You might sneak back more than yus should. Yus know how's that," the Pile said as if both of them know what he is talking about.

"Well sir, you know more than you let on. I am only returning with stories and masgoi writings about Nigmag history. I am expecting a friend to be here by now. Has he come by?"

Pallet is not sure what to say; he was not really expecting a friend.

"Nook, nut here or nut passed. Nut seen the rabbit," the Pile answered annoyingly.

"Why are you here?" asks Pallet.

"Just a keeper… just a keeper. Don't need, don't want, to know. Better this way… no change, no change… don't want to think," the pile said with a tone of defeat.

"But change is the grease, the essence, of life," Pallet replies, eager to change the conversation.

"No change, no change, no grease."

"You've been here too long. So, my name is Pallet from Signigtog. What's your name and where are you from?"

"Tooelep, and here."

"Tooelep! That's an odd name!"

"Odder than Pallet?"

Tooelep is used to people with prying questions.

Pallet has no answer, so he asks again. "Why are you here?"

As Tooelep turns in the faint light, Pallet sees he has an unusual face; a face with a coarse grit sandpaper surface. He has been told he could have trouble with people like this.

"What were you told to do?

"Did what iss told. Was told did fine."

Tooelep speaks like he knows it all and doesn't want to be bothered any more than he has to be.

"Well, I wus to not move til I sees the shit in their eye."

Pallet is aggravated with the keeper. He picks up his belongings and then he sees the keeper has moved. He is not so imposing anymore.

"…gtjipoingn, gtjipoingn, gtjipoingn…," says someone to the left of Pallet.

Pallet knows by now not to be surprised. He turns and sees a middle aged man, who continues to say, "…gtjipoingn, gtjipoingn, gtjipoingn…"

Pallet says, "Goee," but there is no response.

He introduces himself.

"…gtjipoingn, gtjipoingn, gtjipoingn, gtjipoingn…," is all the man says.

Pallet walks toward the man and sees a small campfire in front of him. Despite being so focused, he acknowledges Pallet by nodding toward him. Pallet nods back.

After the acknowledgement, the man says: "…million, million, million, million…"

Occasionally, the man places a pebble on a pile of stones that is part of a mountain as far as the eye can see. The fire is touching the base of the mountain.

"…million, million…"

Pallet attracts Tooelep's attention and nods toward the man. Pallet shrugs his shoulders to show he doesn't understand. He has seen many things in his short life, but this is new to him. Why would someone keep repeating the same word over and over again? The man is able to speak, but will not speak to Pallet.

Tooelep seems disinterested and looks the other way, but they can still see each other.

Tooelep says, "He's the tallyer."

"Tallyer?"

"He keeps tally of Nigmag generosity."

Pallet again shrugs his shoulders indicating he doesn't understand.

"Tallys in the millions now. Gtjipoingn, that's all I hear. Ovel and ovel and again. Gashish. Break me or give me one."

Pallet has never seen anything like this. The man keeps repeating "million" and won't talk to him.

Pallet calls back to Tooelep, "I don't understand. I don't know what's going on here. Can you tell me what's going on?"

"Aaaaa… shib shab. Nigmag generosity, Nigmag generosity," said Tooelep looking at the ground for something that is not there. "Don't pay me tention. Just never the mind."

Pallet isn't sure what to say. He still doesn't understand and is running out of questions. Maybe a mild threat will work.

"You really got an attitude. There's going to be changes here."

"Do what yus gota do. Yus borrowed nickel. I don't kiss ass and tell."

"Smells like it." Pallet is getting better at this sarcasm.

"Aaa… shab. Shib shab. I don't give a ga ga ga goddam. It's all ga ga ga goddam as far as I'm ga, ga, ga, goddam concerned."

Tooelup opens his mouth as if to growl and displays his one good tooth. It stands like a rotting totem pole: wings tipped, nose broken, dead, and ready to fall. Tooelup stops listening to Pallet, and starts writing on the ground.

Pallet watches with interest and says to himself: "It's code writing. He must know the code."

Pallet moves directly in front of Tooelup and asks, "What are you writing?"

"Oigatigentjitjel." [little notes]

"It's good to have notes."

Tooelep doesn't say anything more. Like a disinterested child, he continues to scribble on the ground. He then stops and kicks off his shoes and carefully removes his socks. The bad smell is big enough to kill mosquitos for the distance of a whole day's walking.

Pallet closes his mouth and mumbles, "Close the door. You should have a shaman look at those things. Your toe nails are so big they look like cloven hooves."

"Sapose you's got yus own set clovis hooves, the way you talk and walk; pedicure and all," Tooelep said without looking at Pallet.

Pallet has met his match. There is no way to get the last word on Tooelep. Feeling defeated, he turns away and then sees a motorbike lying by the side of the road.

"Nice bike," he says to Tooelep. "Get much chance to put the testicles on the tank and just go?"

"Aaah… shab. Shib shab," is all Tooelep replies.

He returns to his scribbling. He has had enough of Pallet. He seems to blank out.

As Pallet walks away, he hears Tooelep say, "Countin' wages, countin' wars, countin' births and deaths. Countin' not so friendly governments that Nigmag land has fed. He's a hundred years behind. Be countin' for time too long."

Pallet nods a thank-you towards Tooelep. He is perplexed about how to continue, about where to enter. The place has a keeper, but is unprotected. Tooelep is not informative. He is too cryptic. He doesn't seem to care either way. He seems mostly just pleased with himself for his questions and comebacks. He certainly seems proud of himself and his rotting totem pole of a tooth.

But despite the uncertainty of the situation, there is protocol to follow. Pallet offers Tooelep some nuts, chewberries, and sweet flag root to settle his stomach in case he overeats. Pallet feels certain he will not be refused entry to the portal if he makes an offering to the keeper.

"I was not refused when I first came through, so why would I be refused now," Pallet mutters as if to convince himself he is doing the right thing.

He has entered the stone portal without seeking anyone's permission except his own. He's not sure how that happened, but that doesn't matter now.

Pallet leaves some gifts for the tallyer even though he doesn't understand who the tallyer is and what he is doing.

"He seems to have some connection to Tooelep and to the portal. They are both difficult to understand. Maybe I'll learn later on."

Outside the portal, the day is getting lighter but inside it's getting darker. Outside, the fog is lifting; inside, the shadows are gathering close together making a thick blanket of darkness. The shadows get in each other's way as they rush to conceal what the sun tries to show.

Pallet feels a whirlwind of fear as he walks further into the portal. He slowly turns around and takes 360-degree mental photos. He feels he has to be careful although there are no signs of danger. Disregarding his grandmother's advice, he looks back and sees the keeper sitting down, eating the chewberries and nuts. He is mumbling as he eats. He is like Uncle Soon who also mumbles as he eats.

In between chews, the keeper mumbles, "Dry falls." He eats with the alertness of a cat ready to devour a field mouse.

The advice of his grandmother was to not spend time looking back because the future is the next breath of air... the next meal. Before he looks away, he sees the portal disappear. All that is left is the keeper. Should he turn back? No. He is now interested in what this direction, this new future, has to offer.

Pallet now feels he is being watched but he doesn't see anyone when he looks around. New places make him wary. All he sees is how quickly the shadows are moving to conceal everything. Quickly, he rushes into the bushes to gather firewood, but it is too dark and all he is able to gather are some broken branches. He returns to the clearing and builds a fire.

He gets four sticks from his bag: a drill stick, a bow stick with string, and two flat sticks of different sizes. He puts the larger flat piece on the ground, stands the drill stick on it, wraps the bow string around the drill stick, and with the small flat piece, holds the drill firm and straight. With the bow moving rapidly forward and backward, the drill stick rotates and generates enough heat on the ground stick to make a fire.

Pallet loves the drilling and the fast motion of the sticks. He presses hard on the stick. He is divining for fire. His hunger and the cool evening make him press harder. As quick as a stone can wink, he has a small fire going, just big enough for him to set up camp. He builds a small anapiigan [shelter] near the fire. From the fire he makes a gonus light – a torch – and gathers as much firewood as he easily can find.

With the fire burning well, he sits down inside the anapiigan and takes a wooden cup he has made for drinking tea from his bag. It was his first attempt at making a cup. His friends thought it was ugly and wouldn't touch it, but Pallet is fond of it. He carries ten pebbles that he uses to make his tea. He places the pebbles near the fire. When they are hot, he lifts them with a forked stick and drops them into his cup. The hot pebbles heat the water and steep the tea. Sometimes before heating them, he rubs the pebbles in his palms to give his tea a saline taste. Along with the tea, he makes a meal of nuts and chewberries, which bring back good memories of gathering the blueberries, crushing them in a bowl, and spreading them out for drying. The delicious fruit leathers that are left are the Nigmag's chewberries.

During the night, the fire burns down and goes out. Frost settles in. Pallet sleeps with his head under his blanket, curled up in a small island of body heat. In the morning, everything is covered with a layer of frost. He thinks of the wise saying; "It's not good to pass wind on a cold night." Pallet lays still. Maybe someone will make the fire, maybe the sunlight will warm up the anapiigan, maybe he'll wait for global warming. But he can't wait; he has to get going. He gets up, looks around, and sees a wide river that he doesn't know. But he does know the gathering is in Menagoesg, which is south, so all he has to do is follow the river downstream until he gets his bearings or meets someone who knows the way. As he looks for wood to start a fire, he sees the outline of his sleeping position, as if an angel has fallen and left the impression on the ground. He looks around and sees where Tooelup sat last night. Pallet knows he would have something to say about the angel.

"More like a dead angel."

"Yeah Tooelep, what do you know? You can only count to a dozen."

CHAPTER 7

In his fourth winter after leaving home, Pallet travels the northwestern region of Nigmag Tlaagati. He likes the direction he is going. He feels his snowshoes are taking him somewhere. He likes travelling by snowshoe. The sound of the snowshoes meeting snow means Pallet is now going somewhere. It is here, in the northwest territory of Gespiag, that he meets Gionig.

* * * * *

Pallet comes to a large lake surrounded by spruce covered mountains. In the middle of the lake is an island covered with fir, spruce, and a few maples. "It's an odd place for an island," he thinks, "but nature takes its course and does what it has to do."

He stands on the edge of the frozen lake. The ice feels firm. The winter has been cold and the ice is thick. Except for a few open places where a brook flows in, the lake is frozen solid. He looks at the island and can see that long before human memory, it had once been in the middle of a river. The island has a tail end and a rounded forehead, which shows how it was shaped by the flow of water. He heads towards the tail end of the island. Maybe he will find a cave where he can rest for a few days. Otherwise, he will make camp near the woods where he will be sheltered from the wind. He moves cautiously forward; he is not sure why. Maybe it is the openness of the lake. There are no tracks anywhere, so he has no reason to worry.

From instinct, he looks as far ahead as he can. In the whiteness of the snow and ice, it is difficult to see tracks or any other signs of life. But as he nears the island, he is startled to see blood stained snow. He looks for signs but there are no visible tracks, just a bloodstain. He looks for signs of a struggle. "Maybe two animals had a fight here or maybe an animal dragged itself here.

Maybe it is the remains of an after-birth." He is puzzled but he knows something happened here.

Cautiously, he assesses the situation. The blood looks peculiar and out of place. Maybe it is blood from the air, but who would bleed from the air except birds? He stands straight and quiet. He is certain of three things: it is cold; there is red blood on white snow; the winter wind is whistling through the evergreen trees on the island.

There are no telltale signs of what happened, no signs that tell the story. Then, suddenly, he smells smoke from a wood fire. With this new sign he now knows someone is here even though they are still unseen. Cautiously and gratefully he walks towards the western sun and soon sees a birchbark oitoôm near the end of the island. Tall spruce trees surround the fire, sheltering it from the wind.

He calls a Nigmag greeting, "Goee!" The greeting is to signal he means no harm and that he is there as a friend.

A short figure clothed in rabbit skins emerges from the wigwam and responds with, "Eptjilaasi," an invitation to enter.

A cordial air grows between the two men as introductions are made and cautious defenses dissipate. Pallet's new friend is called Gionig. They come to feel at ease with each other. They both know it is an odd place to meet someone. If a person is far removed from other people, there is a reason. They are both elated to have company. Pallet shares some of his nuts and dried berries. They eat porcupine that Gionig has prepared.

Gionig soon begins to tell the story of how he got here. He begins with a brief history of one of the characters he had encountered. There had been a disagreement between Malsem, Glooscap's brother, and Gionig. He has been waiting for a long time to tell his story. The story just bubbles out with saliva forming a little white beard around his mouth.

"Well first, we all know, everyone in the world knows who Malsem and Glooscap are. Everyone knows them, right? Right. Just to help, here is a little reminder; they were piaminigmag, born of an earth mother. Their father was the day walker who walks across the sky

48

each day. Piaminigmag, they're everywhere. You just don't always see them. They are mixed parentage between gods or spirits and above-ground dwellers. Odd mix, but I guess everyone has a lonesome night. And like most of these rare births, there weren't any witnesses. Big surprise. Right? At the time of their births the twins wanted to eclipse each other. They were competitive even before they were born. It's rumoured they even wrestled while inside their mother's womb. That must have been tough; they couldn't face each other in such close quarters.

"Now Glooscap was born first and loved his mother. Not to be out done, Malsem, the second born, performed an internal cesarean and exited his mother's womb through the spine, killing her instantly. He landed on his feet, wiped them off, and began to walk away. I'm not sure, but my guess is his first step was more of a dance, maybe a rabbit dance. I don't know.

"As soon as possible, the twins separated. They made all efforts to avoid each other. They would make camp on the opposite ends of a mountain range. They both possessed a power that could be used to influence the good or the bad, to manipulate forces by super-human strength, a deadly mix if you ask me. Both could also resort to trickery to gain advantage. Each one could morph into a dwarf or into a nanoid. You couldn't tell who was who. They could change shape and spy on the other, so both were leery of visitors of any shape or size. A barking raven could be one of the twins spying on the other.

"Both have present day followers, the quick to follow type, if you know what I mean; people who can influence the forces to win lotteries and bingo – oooh, they love their bingo and other games of chance. But it was the Malsem followers who achieved the most personal gain from their connection with him. The followers of Malsem the Dark – they are both dark, if you ask me – had no difficulty, none whatsoever, taking advantage of their followers among the Nigmag and other Oapenaagi folks. For the piaminigmag, it was a sign of prestige, looking after yourself first, that sort of thing. With many followers, it was all about personal gain; what's in it for me?

"For the Glooscap followers they found advantage in how often they could help their community. A little self-help along the way doesn't hurt either, right? It was almost boring being a Glooscap follower because personal gain was accomplished by helping others. But they could live with this; this was fine with them.

"As obnoxious youths, the twins grew fast. One blink and they're in moss diapers. With the next blink they're prancing around in their loincloths. Their grandmother, the creator, bless her generous soul, took care of them after their birth – the great parturition they liked to call it. But Malsem was eager to leave and explore the world. Unknown to them at first, they did not need to stay with their grandmother because they had the ability to manipulate the energy of natural and human forces. They were both an uncanny mix of the bad and the good – now that's a deadly combination! But neither one realized, at first, they had this power; the easy to see is not always the easiest to see. Then, Malsem disappeared in the fourth hard winter moon. He disappeared and did not return. Good riddance to bad rubbish, I'd say. His family looked for him, but they knew that he could survive anywhere.

"Like his mother, Glooscap loved his grandmother and stayed with her. His instincts were to take care of his grandmother and his fellow Nigmag. He would teach them how to survive with nature and family."

Gionig pauses in his story as if to add further explanation or ask for a pardon.

"You'll have to excuse me, I've been cooped up too long. I can get carried away."

"Not too far away, I hope." Pallet says, showing real interest.

Gionig continues his story. "While travelling, I came upon an island at the same time Malsem arrived on it. There was immediate disagreement between us. Each of us got our back up over the territory like two puppies with tails pointing at the sky. The conflict was over who could establish a camp here. Unknowingly we had made camps on opposite ends of the island. It was the morning smoke that revealed our camps. Such a disagreement should have been played down as we both want to preserve our power for battles that are sure to ensue between piaminigmag. Normally, we would have had a heated exchange without coming to blows. But, like with the piaminigmag, our blows were close by and ready to fly.

"We locked eyes and the battle began; it began mildly, testing each other, and then advanced to a steady volley of violence. The battle raged for one winter moon with neither of us blinking. Thunder flew, fireballs burned, mountains were thrown down, river water fell like rain, and energy balls burst. The battle reshaped the island. It grew smaller. Running out of things to hurl, Malsem threw a sleeping beaver towards me. Upon awakening, the beaver, in surprise and fright, instinctively defended himself and bit the first thing he saw which was my arm. I quickly grabbed my arm to stop the bleeding, but it was too late. Like a roar of thunder, a drop of my blood hit the snow and the battle was done. The red flag was raised.

"Surrender is swift in these ethereal battles, and conditions were rapidly discussed under the red flag of surrender. I was told I could not leave the island by canoe, or by swimming or flying. I could not use the ice to leave the island nor could breathe to leave the island. I was trapped on the island. The island had become my prison and it was my word that kept me here. I had agreed to the conditions. My isolation has already lasted many hard winter moons."

On hearing the conditions of Gionig's surrender, Pallet asks if he wants to leave the island. If so, Pallet says, he has a plan; he can tie him to a rope and pull him underwater through the frozen-over lake. He can pull him along so he will not have to swim. Gionig is afraid of drowning. He says drowning is not one of his dreams. Pallet tells him not to worry because he knows how the old Nigmag revived drowning victims. Gionig wants to leave the island, so he agrees. Pallet tells him to stay put and he will make a camp on the shore across from the island. He assures him that he'll set everything up. Both spend a worrisome night. They can see each other's campfire, which is reassuring. Each has doubts about the plan but they do not express them.

Pallet captures a beaver that has a hut nearby. He digs a hole in the top of the hut and hauls out the beaver. He takes the beaver to the island and ties a leather rope around its leg. Then he takes the beaver to a place of open water and releases him. The beaver makes a beeline to his hut. Pallet recaptures him and unties the rope. He thanks the beaver and lets it go. Now he has a rope under the ice all the way to the island.

Pallet walks to the island and gives final instructions and encouragement to Gionig. He makes sure he consents to the plan. Gionig says, "Yes."

Gionig hesitates before entering the frigid water, thinking all the while, "Do I trust this stranger? He has no special powers. All he has are nuts and dried berries. The only thing between us is the Nigmag connection. He is Nigmag and I am part Nigmag. Well, it's worth a try; probably better than my present fate."

He steps into the water, which shows no mercy and immediately covers his feet. "Masgoi, this water is cold! Who needs this anyway? I'll just spend the rest of the time on the island. No rush, right?"

The frigid water stings like a basket full of bees. He wades further in. The water is up to his bellybutton, then to his neck.

"Why did I listen to Pallet; who is he anyway?"

The cold water sends a panic message. He is in shock, but before he can change his mind, he loses consciousness. Gionig slips quietly under the ice.

Pallet runs across the lake and grabs the rope, He plants his feet and begins to pull. He pulls fast but the rope hits a snag. Pallet swears, "Masgoi!" Maybe he's caught on a rock or on one of the old trees on the lake bottom. The rope has not broken, so they are still good. Pallet releases the tension on the rope. He tugs a bit and it pulls freely. Again, he pulls Gionig as quickly as possible along under the ice.

"It's good the lake doesn't have much of a current. It would have been impossible to pull him along against a strong current."

As he pulls the line, he doesn't feel any struggle; it's like a dead fish on a line. Pallet chases the thought away. He pulls the rope as fast as he can. He secures his footing as the pulling gets harder.

"He must be close," Pallet says to himself.

Finally, Pallet sees a rabbit fur coat at the end of his rope. He grabs Gionig by the leg and turns him around to get hold of his arms. He pulls him up without a struggle. A cloud of worry comes to his mind. He drags him to the bank. Gionig is not moving. Pallet climbs up the shore as fast as he can and drags Gionig close to his big campfire. He dries him off and wraps him in a dry rabbit fur coat. Gionig is breathing like a stone.

"Thank the creator that stones cannot drown. They can hold their breath forever."

Pallet hangs Gionig head side up from a tree close to the fire to keep him warm.

Before the daring escape, Pallet had prepared a tightly sewn up seal bladder and filled it with smoke from his fire. He attached a hollow stick at the open end and plugged it. He now opens the rabbit fur coat, rubs seal grease on the end of the hollow stick, takes out the plug, and inserts it into Gionig's anus.

While waiting for the results, Pallet fetches some mud from the beaver hut, covers a partridge he has snared, and places it in the fire.

"It should be ready by the time he comes to."

He sits by the fire and looks at Gionig. The smoke should now be travelling up his intestines. Pallet watches for smoke to emerge from his mouth and nostrils. Soon, Gionig begins coughing up smoke and water. Pallet cuts him down, lays him near the fire, and covers him. He sleeps there for the rest of the day.

"You never know what a fumal enema will do," Pallet thinks with a sense of relief.

Later, when Gionig stirs and rouses a bit, Pallet says, "You look pretty well done."

"Well… done… is… a… good… word." Gionig replies, making a great effort to say each word.

"Rest some more."

"Yes… rest…" Gionig dozes off.

CHAPTER 8

The gentanteget lash Taapoategl's wrists and ankles together, jam a long pole between her legs and arms, and pick her up where she hangs with her head slung back like a dead deer. They start walking. They move fast, half running. They stop only long enough to change carriers.

Taapoategl's wrists and ankles chafe badly against the pole and start to bleed. They stop and untie her. One of the gentanteget tosses her on his shoulder and starts off at a fast walk. Her stomach begins to hurt. She struggles, which forces them to stop. She bends forward and walks around to relieve the pain. She motions that she will walk. She doesn't move fast enough, so they carry her again.

Taapoategl is confused by their speed. They move quickly with great determination. They do not speak. They just keep moving. With the sack over her head, she can't tell anything about where they are or where they are going.

Again, she indicates she'll walk. They tie a rope around her neck to pull her along more quickly, half running, half walking. She has a difficult time breathing through the tight sack. When she hesitates, a gentanteget jerks the rope and pulls her forward. She stumbles on, feeling lost in the darkness of the sack.

They keep moving all day and stop late at night. They give her dried venison to eat. They do not make a fire but instead huddle near a large fallen log. Taapoategl is tied to a tree with some slack on the rope. She gathers spruce bows to sleep on. She curls up and tucks her head inside her cloak; the warmth of her breath and the thought of her mother's patience when she made the cloak, helps her fall asleep.

They start travelling again before daylight on the third day. The gentanteget are now more animated. They talk and laugh. They rarely stop to rest. They rest while walking by going at a slower pace. They stop twice to drink from a brook. As the day wears on, they stop to rest less and less. When Taapoategl resists the fast pace, she is struck on her back. When night comes, they continue walking, although at a slower pace. They travel all night as if there was a deadline to meet.

Suddenly, in the dark of the night, Taapoategl smells smoke. A strange feeling of comfort comes over her. For a moment, she thinks it may be a Nigmag settlement or the camp of some Nigmag who are passing through on their way to share provisions with the next village or just to visit. She listens for familiar sounds like the way voices echo from people talking in an oigoôm, but she hears nothing.

"Maybe they are still sleeping," she thinks, "After all, it's still early."

She makes plans to alert them. She knows the Nigmag words that can be heard at a long distance, and these words are a signal of distress. She'll wait for an opportune time to call out the long distance heard words, the echo words. The Nigmag will mobilize once they hear her distress call. She goes over the words in her mind; "Oetjgooen." This is to ask if they're coming. Like a barking raven answering another raven in the middle of winter, the Nigmag would reply, "Oetjgoei," I am coming.

The smell of smoke grows stronger and her anticipation grows. Soon she will pretend to fall, rip the sack from her head, and call for help. Then, she hears a woman's voice but it's not a comfort. Taapoategl doesn't understand her but knows she is speaking the language of the cousins, the people who come from across the ocean and are taking over Nigmag land.

They have arrived at one of the cousin's homesteads. The woman has been expecting the hunters and a meal is ready. They are happy to see each other. The cabin is warm. The sack is removed from Taapoategl's head. She is given food and a seat near the fireplace. She looks around the room and sees a shiny metal cross on which there is a figure with a sad downtrodden face. Hanging next to the cross is something she has never seen before; it looks like a sack with a rack of strange moose horns attached to it. After she has eaten, Taapoategl is locked in a backroom built into a hillside like a root cellar. Light from the main room shines under the door and through cracks in the boards. She finds a straw bed with a ragged blanket. She lies down, exhausted, and falls asleep chanting a rhythmic mantra, "Gitjoo… Gitjoo… Gitjoo."

Taapoategl wakes to the sound of people moving around the cabin. At first she is confused but then remembers where she is. The light coming through the cracks in the door plays on walls of her prison. She cries silently and chants, "Gitjoo… Gitjoo… Gitjoo." The chants help her forget where she is but not who she is.

Taapoategl gets up and tries to see through the cracks in the door. She can see the light from the fireplace and smell food cooking. The door opens and the woman places food and water on a nearby bench. Taapoategl eats in the semi-darkness. Later, the woman enters again, ties a long rope around her waist, leads her outside, and ties the other end of the rope to the corner of a shed. The woman motions to Taapoategl to carry firewood from the shed to the house. She follows her instructions, glad to be outside again, but all the while quietly calling for her mother, "Gitjoo… Gitjoo… Gitjoo."

As she begins to move the firewood, she finds pieces of masgoi. The bark is dry and peels easily. She collects the pieces of bark and puts them aside in a corner of the shed. She's not sure what she'll use them for but she has the idea she can write on them.

After carrying in a supply of firewood, Taapoategl remains outside even though the day is cold. She can now see that the cousin's cabin has been built on a hillside at the edge of a clearing with a brook flowing nearby. The rope is long enough to reach the brook. She lies on the bank and leans down to drink. The water is cold and refreshing. She thinks of the water forever flowing, forever running to the ocean; it has a destiny. "What now is my destiny?" She thinks of her family as she washes her face and hands.

"What are they doing now? They must be looking for me."

She explores the area along the brook and finds a small piece of bone the gentanteget had thrown out. She sharpens one end by rubbing it on a rock.

"This is will be perfect for writing on masgoi."

She drinks again from the brook and again washes herself. The water is cold, but the cleansing is important to her.

Suddenly, one of the gentanteget comes running towards the cabin, grabs Taapoategl and rushes her into the backroom. He ties a cloth around her mouth and ties up her hands and feet. She can't move. She breathes lightly and focuses on hearing. Two other men enter the cabin. A conversation follows and they stay for sometime. She doesn't understand what they are talking about. Just before they leave, the door to the backroom is opened and the visitors take a look at Taapoategl.

In the evening, the other gentanteget return with a good catch of rabbits and partridges. They all eat supper with little conversation and soon retire to their beds for the night. The men leave early in the morning. Taapoategl is given her breakfast and is motioned to clean the house, fetch water, and carry in more firewood.

As the days go by, the woman makes sure Taapoategl is well fed. She keeps her outside as much as possible, which Taapoategl clearly prefers. The outside is her shelter. From time to time visitors come and she is again rushed into the backroom.

She continues to save masgoi from the woodpile and hides it in the shed. The weather is still cold and the ground is still mostly frozen, but she is able to gather spruce roots where the brook flows out of the woods and erosion has left them exposed. She finds a sharp piece of oaglôspgosoa [quartz] that can also be used to write on masgoi. She hides her tools in the shed.

Taapoategl thinks often about trying to escape and return to her family. But she is not sure where she is or what direction she would go if she did escape. She is sure her family must be looking for her. They could easily have seen what had happened when she was captured. They could follow the trail and come to rescue her.

If she escaped, the gentanteget would immediately come after her. Even if she managed to get away, it would be hard to survive on her own in the woods. Her only hope is that her family will find her. With this thought always in mind, Taapoategl does the work she is told to do and pretends to be content with her situation. The woman notices her submissive manner and eventually stops tying her to the rope when she goes outside. Taapoategl makes no effort to escape and performs her tasks even better than before, all the while waiting for her family to find her. The woman is pleased and thinks how valuable this captive will be when the opportunity comes to strike a deal.

CHAPTER 9

Pallet has set traps and snares in the woods surrounding their camp. He has seen plenty of deer and moose tracks but this is no time to deal with big game. For just the two of them there is plenty of small game. He has already picked up a rabbit from one of his snares, and then just missed getting a partridge. He has a long pole with a leather string that reaches from one end to the other. The light end has a loop, with which he can snare birds, but this time the partridge startled before Pallet could snag it off the limb of a spruce tree. The bird quickly flew while Pallet's hunger stayed with him.

"This rabbit will have to do for now."

He returns to camp where he finds Gionig sitting near the fire.

"Good morning."

"Good morning."

"Made it through!" Pallet says with a feeling of relief.

"Made it through… made it through," replies Gionig in a weak voice. "Any nuts left?"

"Sure, help yourself."

Pallet sets to dressing out the rabbit, careful to not tear the hide, which will be good for making repairs on their winter coats. He offers a prayer to the rabbit and buries its entrails in the snow for other animals and birds. He saves everything that can be eaten.

There is solemnness between Gionig and Pallet. They are both feeling the effects of what they had accomplished. Gionig doesn't move from his place near the fire. Both men are unusually quiet. They know they have defied the odds. They are now wary of what might come of it. They speak only in low tones, unsure whether to laugh or not. They are alert to everything around them.

Pallet props up the rabbit over the fire with a long stick that has a cross piece at the end where the rabbit is attached in a spread eagle position. While the rabbit is cooking, he cleans the skin and stretches it on a circular wood frame. He places the frame near the fire so the skin will dry and can be packed for travelling.

Gionig watches quietly as Pallet goes about his chores. They both look across the frozen water to the island that has been Gionig's prison for many hard winter moons.

"It's strange," Gionig says in a low voice. "I was there so long I now almost miss the place. It's hard to understand but that's all I knew for a long time."

Pallet sees the large stretch of clear ice past the island and says, "Good place to have an ice game."

"Where?" asks Gionig.

Pallet silently points his lips toward the open area and then says; "Yes, a very good place. I'll bet there are many Nigmag hooks in the nearby woods. There's an open field to hold celebrations and a wooded area for shelter from the river winds. Yes, this would be a good place for the ice game. Do know the story of the ice game?"

Gionig looks at the rabbit; it looked more appetizing than a story right now. He thinks, "Well, that's how it is… sometimes, the best stories are told before a meal."

Before he could say anything, Pallet begins his story.

"Maybe this is where they had the big tournament. I think they called it the temple cup. Have you heard about this metal cup? The Nigmag played a tournament for it much earlier in our history. One of the early visitors from across the ocean left it here for safekeeping. This is a story I heard from my grandfather. He was known for making the best ice sticks, the Nigmag hook. People said your chance of winning a tournament increased if you had one of his sticks."

Pallet enjoys talking about the ice game tournament; he's now really into it.

"Long ago, the lost ship people from across the ocean began arriving in our Nigmag land; some came with gifts and trade items; some came looking for unimaginable riches in minerals, furs, seafood, or slaves. There was one seeker who came with a precious goblet. It fit the hand well and had a red stain on the inside, maybe something like cranberry juice. Goblet seekers who had a similar high regard for the cup were pursuing him. Already the idea of pursuit gave the cup some mystery. Besides the pursuit, there was not much else to the cup. It could have been a cup you left at a waterhole, a communal cup of sorts. Contrary to rumour, you could not store maple sap in it. And for secret reasons the container had to be protected forever and should never be allowed to fall into the 'wrong hands.' Wrong hands? Who could have wrong hands? One had right and left hands, but 'wrong hands?'

"Anyway, the visitor insisted that the cup had a history of immense honour. To humour the visitor's wishes, the Nigmag agreed to safeguard the goblet, and it was decided that the cup would remain under protection in Tlaagati until such time when it was safe for it to return across the ocean.

"The next order of business was to decide which among the many Nigmag districts would have the honour of keeping this cup safe. How would they decide? Different contests were proposed: an inter-district game of oaltesg, a weapon demonstrating ability, and an oratory session? No consensus could be reached so no decision was made. In the mean time, the grand sagamao was handed the cup for safekeeping. The decision was to be made by the end of the long winter moon overhead. The chief gave the visitor a Nigmag hook with instructions to bring the hook back when he or a representative returns for the goblet. The hook was decorated with an intricate double curve symbol, which represents two people standing as one, back to back with arms spread to give and accept the generosity of life.

"The season moved on and the winter winds returned. People cut holes in the ice to fish, and to spear eels. Spearing eels in the winter was a delight. You would make a hole in the ice about a yard in diameter. The spear was a long pole with a forked end. You began at the centre of the hole and repeatedly jabbed the spear into the muddy river bottom where the eels buried themselves. Once struck, the eel would curl around the spear and could be hauled onto the ice. The spear fisher would continue to spear around the hole extending the fishing area as far as the pole would reach. It was like fishing blind.

"The ice game players had to play further up river so as not to disturb the fishers. Many of them were frequent and skillful ice game players. The time was close for the Nigmag ice game tournament and the players were getting ready. They practiced running on the ice. They went looking for the perfect curved maple stick. The Nigmag hook was a kind of magic wand. New growth shoots from fallen maple trees made the best sticks. The stick was like a cane and required practice to be skilled in its use. Some liked their stick a little flat to cover more ice and give more control of the wooden disk, while others liked a sharp curl at the bottom of the stick. The disk could be flipped up and dropped with these curled sticks. The curled stick made it easier to hook someone who had broken loose with the disk from the pack. There were stick-makers who guarded their chosen hook territory where they snipped and bent and shaped future Nigmag hooks. Some players hired the best experts in hook making that Tlaagati had. Today we would say they had bonsai hook gardens. Secretive stuff. You had to know someone to enter these stick gardens.

"The Nigmag from Signigtog had won the past two tournaments and the smart wager was on them, but the loosing Oomanaagi team was getting better each year. With tournaments like this there could always be surprise winners as well. Surprise winners were called 'the short sticks.'

"The team from Signigtog had lost their two best players. Actually, they were banned from community activities because they had raped a young girl during one of the games. They were related to the leader, and probably felt they had immunity. It was reported to the grand council of the Nigmag and the two were found guilty. They were banned until further notice.

"The twelfth moon was approaching and many women and men were preparing. Team members were chosen according to their skill. Those who were sure footed on ice were chosen first. Some made devices to get better traction. In these competitions, every advantage was looked for. Despite all the tricks, the old timers said it was in the toes. Each team needed a minimum of ten players with spares who would substitute if there were an injury. The games would last a half a day without a break no matter the weather. Neither rain, sleet, snow or cold could stop the game. The winning team went on to play the next winning team.

"Of all the players, Sitamogtjitj was the one to watch. He would plant himself near the goal and no one would be able to move him. Among the women players, Gonteetj was dangerous on the runway. Her mother was from the bear clan, and Gonteetj ran on the ice like she had claws on her feet. The players would tease her and ask what she was doing there; shouldn't she be hibernating by now? She sure could run and turn on the ice.

"The time came to play and rumours were flying left and right about who had the best team. The district chiefs were meeting to renew ties and bragging rights. Before the meeting ended, the grand chief suggested that the team who won this year would safeguard the cup. There was no opposition, and the news spread pretty fast. Each district was now playing for the goblet. It was a four-day tournament with last year's winner getting a bye. On the first day, there were two games with winners advancing. The second day had one game. On the third day, the team that had gotten the bye played a team from the first game. The second game was from the winners of game two. And the winners of third day advanced to the fourth day, when the championship game was played.

"The games were followed with many festivities: food, dancing, and rowdiness. What's a Nigmag gathering without some rowdiness? In the evening, the bang and thump of the oaltesg game could be heard as the maple burl bowl struck the ground and the bone dice flew through the air and landed on the ground. Some players were able to influence the game by waving their hand over the dice and changing how they would land.

"The traders also brought their wares: gloves, fish line and hooks, moccasins, ice sticks, bear grease salve for treating bruises and sprains; you name it, it could be traded there. The Shamans set up sweat lodges around the edge of the gathering. Nothing like a religious ceremony to renew visions during the ice game! Each player prayed for safety and fair play, and absolutely no one prayed for victory. Next to oaltesg, the ice game was the Nigmag national game. With so much activity, the whole Nigmag economy was in full swing. This was the time to trade and consume. The traders urged, 'consume, consume, you weary devils.'

"The tournament moved swiftly and, as predicted, Signigtog and Oomanaagi were in the finals. It snowed but that did not stop the game. Extra maple disks were on hand in case of breakage. The Oomanaagi team was quick to score first, but the bigger Signigtog team regained the lead and kept it for the rest of the game. Both teams lost players that were injured by the curved maple sticks or by the hard, slippery surface. The Signigtog team was given the goblet and did a victory dance. After that year, the cup was never seen again. Stories were told and retold that the goblet is still waiting for the owner to return with the Nigmag hook.

"There were people who came to look for the goblet, but it was never found again. Truth be known, it was the losing team who actually got the cup. It was a diversion to safeguard it. To further guard the cup, it was covered in masgoi with information inscribed on the outer surface about its history. It was written in Gômgoetjoigasigel [Nigmag writing system]. Also included, along with the goblet, was a record of the historic events that had taken place thus far. Family names were included, marriages, births, and deaths. To the Nigmag, this information was more valuable than the cup. Taagô"

After the story, Pallet and Gionig split the meaty hindquarters of the rabbit and nibble the backbone and the skin covering the chest cavity. They wrap the front quarters in birchbark; this will make another meal if they are unable to soon find more food.

CHAPTER 10

When Taapoategl is outside she lets her mind wander. This is the only part of her that is free. Everything else seems immobilized. In her captive life there is no change. The trees are still there, the brook is still there, and the bars of light through her backroom door are still there. She has time to think. She thinks about the strange feeling of living half underground. She is not sure what to make of it, but she is still glad to be breathing. There is an enclosed routine to her life and she is almost glad there is no change.

For now, she lives with the hope that her family will find her and bring her home. This is the first and last thought of her day – her family. She wants to tell them how sorry she is and that she will be glad get her own switch.

"Mesgei Gitjoo. Mesgei Gitjoo." [I'm sorry, Mother. I'm sorry Mother.] This is all she can say.

A light rain is steadily falling as Taapoategl sits in the shed doorway. Like a poem on masgoi, her life is in front of her. The trees are there, the brook is there, and bars of light in the backroom door are still there. She likes the rain falling on her hands and face. At first the drops sting like small needles but the sensation soon disappears and her face is covered with raindrops. She doesn't understand why people always cover up when it rains. As the rain falls, it awakens a special awareness and stirs her shaken life. The dampness of the air awakens the smells of the earth; the smells of fallen, decomposing leaves, broken branches, pine needles, seeds lying dormant, ready to burst into growth at the earliest opportunity.

As the rain falls, the shed becomes an accumulation of earthy smells. The shed has an earth floor on which wood chips, pieces of bark, and dead leaves have accumulated and decomposed. Taapoategl finds this smell enjoyable like the smell of planting a garden, gathering medicine, or digging for worms. All these sensory memories are generated by the smell of the earth.

Then, beyond the surface smells, there is another faint odour that Taapoategl cannot identify although she has smelled it before. The smell lingers on the periphery of the doorway where she is sitting. She inhales deeply to capture more of the smell. Suddenly, the smell has a pungency that pushes Taapoategl away. She quickly gets up and steps out of the doorway. She walks to a large pine tree on the bank behind the cabin. The fallen needles make a comfortable place to sit. The branches divert the rain and she stays dry.

Taapoategl knows what the smell is. She has no doubt. She has seen the decaying bodies of animals in the woods and recognizes the smell.

She looks over to the shed and says to herself, "Maybe a porcupine or a squirrel died in the shed or maybe an injured bird died in there. Maybe I should find it and bury it outside."

Now, more curious than cautious, Taapoategl wants to see what she smells. She returns to the shed and, with her eyes open like full moons, moves into its dark interior. She is unable to see much in the darkness but is determined to find out what smells so bad. The strength of the odour makes her move cautiously. She doesn't want to step on a dead and rotting rabbit. The smell would stay on her moccasin. Even though she can barely see anything, she looks intently into the darkest corners. She has a sense, even in the dark, where the walls are. She extends her hand forward to avoid bumping into anything, but all she feels is the empty space. She moves further into the darkness, which makes her uneasy but still not ready to retreat. She feels around in the dark corners with her hands with no results.

She stays put to reestablish herself. She stomps the floor with one foot and then the other. She bends both knees and spreads her hands down as if to lighten her weight if she happens to lose her balance and fall on the floor. Her hands touch the cold floor and she retracts them a bit. She establishes a safe distance between her hands and the ground and then glides them over the surface. She moves her hands slowly to avoid cuts or scrapes. Her scan reveals nothing. The rotting odour is now so strong it drowns out her other senses. She is overcome by the need for fresh air. She leaves the shed to catch her breath. Some smells can take away the ability to think clearly.

Once outside, she finds a stick to use as a probe. With some dread, she returns to the shed. She is repulsed by the rotting smell, but for some strange reason is also determined to find its source. She enters the shed and this time stands still waiting until her eyes adjust to the darkness. She wants to be sure of what she sees. As her eyes adjust she can see an outline of the deep interior of the shed. She feels slightly dizzy from bending over and staring so intently. She rubs her eyes for relief and without thinking, glances upward toward the roof. She stares like an owl and notices something beyond the darkness. A faint light creeps into the shed under the roofline at the top of the walls. She stands erect, stretching toward the roofline and the stench gets stronger.

Peering intently through the darkness she now sees a dark shape where the top of the wall meets the roof. She probes it with her stick. By now, she can see more clearly. The dark shape looks like a small log. She moves to the left where there is more light coming under the roofline. She sees a dark ball on top of the shape.

"Maybe it's a porcupine all curled up; or a raccoon. Yes, it is a small animal," she says to herself. "The poor thing must have been seeking shelter from the cold and died."

But she can only guess in the semi-darkness. She pokes her stick at the curled up animal. She likes small animals and she wants to help it or at least make a grave for it. She feels a strong urge to help the poor animal.

Relieved that she has found the source of the smell, Taapaotegl goes outside. She would have been glad to leave the animal alone, but she couldn't shake the feeling of wanting to help it even though it is dead. She breathes hard until all she smells is the fresh air and the stench is gone. After that, she breathes even deeper, gathering and storing air in her lungs. She remembers holding her breath when she went swimming in the summer and looked at all the different fish and plants under the water.

She returns to the shed with her stick. This time she knows what's ahead of her and what she will find. She goes right in, using her stick and her memory to guide her. She comes to the wall where the animal is directly overhead on the top of the log wall. Although her intentions are good, and she knows it is dead, she is still hesitant about disturbing the small animal.

"Maybe it's a baby who lost its way; but that's all the more reason for me to help," she reasons to herself.

Overcoming her misgivings, she pokes at the small animal with her stick. It doesn't move. Another poke and still no movement. She tries pushing it sideways. Suddenly, it slips off the log and falls on the dirt floor. The smell becomes stronger as if angry from having been disturbed. Taapoategl is startled by seeing the size of the animal, now spread out on the floor and magnified in the darkness.

Frightened, she rushes out stumbling and gasping for fresh air. She goes back to the pine tree to recover. A new sense of fear has come over her and she doesn't know why. She feels exhausted by it but challenged and almost exhilarated as well. She has not known this kind of fear before and doesn't know what to do. She breathes deeply; this is all she knows to do. She rises and stands without moving for a long time. She understands where she is and her survival instinct slowly returns.

Taapoategl now feels she has caused a disturbance with her curiosity and must return everything as it was. Perhaps what she disturbed has something to do with a cousins' ritual, maybe with their religion. She has seen the sad metal cross and the strange moose horn bag on display in the cabin.

She remembers her uncle, who used to say, "There are many religions to be had and many best not had, many are best forgotten."

She doesn't totally understand what this means, but she knows she has to respect people who have different religions.

Although confused, Taapoategl is determined. She enters the shed again with her eyes open and her mouth and nose covered. With her stick, she tries to lift the fur back to the top of the log wall, but it falls back and another fur now falls to the ground with the same flop and stench. She now has two animals on the floor.

"Where does this end?" she wonders. "They must be porcupines."

But she can't feel any porcupine quills with her stick. She moves closer and tries to put the second fur back on the log. It slips back. She doesn't give up; she tries again. Her eyes and nose have adjusted to the situation. She moves bravely forward determined to complete her strange task, only to see there are three more furs on the log.

This time it is not the uncertainty or the stench that drives her from the shed, but a disorienting sense of shock and confusing horror. The only recourse that is real for her is to run to the brook. With a deep breath, she plunges her head in the cold water. The shock snaps her back to reality. She slowly withdraws her head and dries it with the inside of her coat. She rubs her face with her hands. As her breathing returns, her fear and anxiety subside.

"I must put those furs back on the log. The gentanteget may get angry if they find out what I have done."

She returns to the shed hoping that the rotting animals will have magically crawled away. They are still there. She moves cautiously in the dark making a semi-circle around them, trying to think of what to do. There is nothing she has learned in her young life that tells her what is now the right thing to do.

"Just put the furs back," she repeats to herself.

Taapoategl pokes at the one of the furs until she can feel it catching on the end of her stick. When she moves backward to lift the fur toward the top of the wall, she steps on a loose stick, which rolls under her foot. She loses her balance and falls backward. The fur flies through the air like a live thing and lands on her stomach. She doesn't move. She is scared the animal will crawl towards her face. It was bad enough trying to return the fur to the log without touching it, but now it's touching her and close to her face. She slides on her back toward the light of the doorway and then sees a strand of dry, green grass woven in the black fur.

"What kind of animal weaves grass in its fur?" Her mind is spinning wildly.

"Maybe it's Potlatamootj, a creature who sometimes mysteriously appears to people when they need help." Her mind is racing.

"You have to be serious with Potlatamootj. He can be a prankster."

Carried away with anticipation, Taapoategl thinks Potlatamootj, has come to grant her two wishes. But she only needs one and will gladly give the other one away to whom ever needs it.

"I must be careful," she thinks, "The Potlatamootj could play a trick on me. They only appear to people who believe in them. Everyone knows that Potlatamootj lives side by side with the Nigmag."

Taapoategl closes her eyes to be sure it is a Potlatamootj. She remembers the rule, "If you see one, close your eyes. If it is still there when you open them, your wishes will be granted."

She opens her eyes and the fur is still on her stomach. She is elated and is sure that her wish will now be granted. She immediately wishes to be returned to her family. Not sure what to do, she closes her eyes again. She listens for the sounds of her family in their camp, maybe of children playing, but there is no sound. Nevertheless she is certain that when she opens her eyes her wish will have come true. She can hardly wait. She hesitates; she wants to savour the anticipation. Tears roll down from her closed eyes. She is so happy. The first thing she will do when she opens her eyes is pick up her masgoi container and run to fetch water. Her family was sleeping when she left, so she knows they will still be sleeping when she returns.

"I have been in a bad dream and am about to wake up."

She opens her eyes and looks for the five oigoôm, the central fire pit, and her belonging-to. But she doesn't see anything, just the dark interior of the shed and the rotting animal on her stomach.

She can't move. The fur on her stomach is holding her down. It is not what she wants to see. But at least the fur is not moving. She gets up on her knees and the fur falls to the ground. With a hand covering her nose and mouth, she gets to her feet and leans unsteadily towards the fur. She now sees that the dry grass has been woven into a braid. Even with her nose blocked, she knows it's tjiensigoo, the tall, sweet smelling grass that the Nigmag gather in the summer time. Not only can she faintly smell it, she can now clearly see it. She leans still closer to make sure it is definitely a woven braid of sweetgrass. She vividly remembers her mother and her aunt often using sweetgrass in religious ceremonies and wearing it as a religious ornament.

"This can't be! What animal has a braid of sweetgrass? Maybe a child, playing with a pet, put it there. Maybe it is a spirit animal that lives among the Nigmag. Spirit animals are given special attention because they can help you in times of dire need." Again, her thoughts are racing, trying to make sense of what she is seeing.

"If it is a spirit animal maybe *it* can help me return home... home and safe... home to belonging-to..." Taapoategl feels the ground slipping away.

Then, without warning, like a spring flood, her Nigmag family washes over her memory. Tears fill her eyes.

"It can't be... it can't be".

She collapses... no sight, no sound, no sense... just darkness.

"My Nigmag weave sweetgrass in their hair."

Overloaded with horror and disbelief, she staggers out of the shed. She doesn't run. Disoriented, she stands outside. She wonders what has happened. She awakens to rain falling on her face. She is lying on the ground. She stays quiet, as if hiding. She feels the ground under her bare legs.

"If I don't move, no one will see me. I am safe here."

A light rain continues. She wants to feel something concrete, something real. A strange sense of calm returns and she realizes the fur is hair.

Half dazed, she re-enters the shed. The dread quickly returns, but she pushes it aside. It doesn't matter now. She has had a lifetime of experience in a few minutes. She picks up the hair with her small hands. She feels the hair; it feels well cared for despite the rotten smell.

She looks toward the open door as if to get a sense of direction. She looks back at the hair and sees a flash of light from the hair. She looks closely and sees a shiny object attached to the sweetgrass.

"Maybe a sea shell, a polished stone, or a piece of shiny metal," she thinks.

She pulls back the hair to see what it is. To her horror, she sees it's a small shiny metal cross, the decoration Nigmag are given when they convert to the cousins' religion.

She screams her aunt's name in silence, "Attaoisoogatiget!"

Taapoategl stands straight as a totem pole waiting for the time it will fall to the ground. She screams again in the same way and her grief pushes the blood from her face. It now hurts to move; she is exhausted. She moves the scalp closer to the light, and she sees a bone needle in the hair.

On the verge of vomiting, Taapoategl crawls out of the shed, finds her way to the brook, and puts her face into the cold water. She opens her eyes and sees small pebbles rolling down the stream; they seem to dance with the music of the water. With her strong lungs, she stays underwater for as long as she can.

"Maybe the water will wash away the horror."

Her lungs feel like they will burst when she finally pulls herself from the water and collapses.

Taapaotegl awakens sitting by the brook, wishing not to believe what she has seen. Still a child, she thinks about the future.

"What is happening? What will happen to me now?"

The sight of the sweetgrass woven into the hair sticks in her mind. The image is indelible; it floods her mind and overflows with emotion. Not knowing what more to do, she splashes her face with cold water and listens.

She hears ravens barking at each other. The barking reminds her there is some reality somewhere. She listens for the leaves but the trees are still bare. She had hoped the sound of leaves would bring her back to reality. She hears the brook, and she finally feels her heart again. She doesn't move; her eyes dart about with no set focus. Her mind reels.

Finally, a thought comes to her that she repeats over and over like a chant; "There are still Nigmag who weave sweetgrass in their hair."

She finds herself back in the shed in front of her aunt's hair. Her bones shake like a thousand shimmering poplar leaves in the summer. Taapoategl falls next to the hair and embraces her aunt's remains. She rises, puts the hair back on the log and leaves the shed.

CHAPTER 11

Yesterday was a day of recovery. This morning they feel better.

"So, are you still with the dead?" Pallet asks. "I know you weren't breathing for a long time. You up to travelling or shall we rest a bit more?"

"I guess the dead don't want you yet; that's a good deal." Pallet is trying to lighten up the seriousness of yesterday. There is concern in his voice. This is uncharted territory for him.

"Should we rest another day?" Pallet repeats.

"I don't remember much… not sure I want to remember… just lots of bubbles, cold bubbles… don't feel so bubbly now." Gionig finally manages to reply.

Gionig is sitting by the fire but he is so glad to be alive it doesn't much matter if he is warm or cold.

Suddenly, he stands, rubs his hands over the fire and speaks up more strongly. "That sure was some experience. I sure can cut the notch off on this one. No matter what, sun or rain, I don't have to do this again. Once is plenty. I'm glad the white light I saw was the sun coming up. After the plunge, I wasn't sure I would ever see the sunrise or the sunset again.

"But I can tell you a thing or two about the dip," he continues in an even more animated way. "It was wet and liberating. I've heard that when people drown and are then revived they have no fear of death or birth – something about beginnings and tragic endings. I know it's hard to believe. I felt I was immersed and drowning in a womb, if anyone remembers what that's like. I was both drowning and not drowning. Suddenly, I felt a tug on the rope. I'm sure glad you were pulling on the rope. I have to think more about all this.

Maybe I shouldn't dwell on it."

Suddenly feeling weak and wobbly, Gionig sits down and stokes the fire as if it needed his attention. He is happy and wants to talk, but the effort has exhausted him.

"Maybe another day's rest and I will be fine, if that is ok with you. It would be hard to travel in this condition."

"Yeah, that's good," Pallet replies.

This was his first experience with a fumal enema. He had heard about it, but didn't know anyone who had actually done it. He wasn't sure how it would turn out, but is glad that Gionig is alive.

Pallet puts several hot stones into a wooden bowl that is filled with water for making rabbit stew. The lean meat of the rabbit will be excellent protein for Gionig at this stage of recovery. At high noon, the stew is done. They both sit quietly by the fire paying full attention to the silence. Pallet chews on the backbone of the rabbit while Gionig drinks the broth.

After their meal, Gionig feels stronger and asks, "Any plans on where you are going next? I have to tell you, this is a strange place to be travelling through. Not many people come here anymore – strange place, strange people. Not much here except the wilderness. Maybe you find a hermit, or someone on a vision quest looking for meaning in their life. Quest your best, I'd say. Sometimes, the simplest things in life are the hardest to find."

"I'm not sure," replies Pallet. "I have been gathering fragments of birchbark that tell something about the Nigmag. A lot of Nigmag history was written on bark. A lot of the bark has survived but a lot probably hasn't. I have collected many pieces but I don't know what they all mean. A lot of bark pieces were confiscated during the conflict between the Nigmag and the cousins."

"Who are the cousins?" Gionig asks.

"They were people who came from across the ocean. Some bark contains information about agreements and some tell about Nigmag history. It was a sad and brutal time. The spineless history books portray it as a cornerstone in the history of Canada, but the real story is a blow to the crotch of Canadian history."

"Whoa...," Gionig speaks up, taken aback.

"Sorry, this history gets me riled up."

Gionig stirs the broth with small twig. "This is good broth you made. It's just what I need."

After a pause, Gionig asks, "Did they write on the bark about the traders?"

"Traders? I don't know. They might have," Pallet replies.

"If they wrote about traders then they may have written about *captaine des sauvages*," Gionig says with some uncertainty.

Pallet feels this statement like a mountain falling from the sky. He has heard of *captaine des sauvages* before, but he hadn't made the connection with the traders.

"Ah yes," Gionig said with a small smile, "...*captaine des sauvages*. They played a crucial, and later an opportunistic part, in the early Nigmag and cousins' history. Who were they? Well let me tell you; they were like you and me, well more like you than me. They were the offspring of Nigmag and cousins' relationships, the result of a few folks meeting in secret. They had one parent who was Nigmag and one parent who was a cousin. They were able to move and mingle in both worlds, the in-betweeners, one could say.

"Anyway, they saw opportunity later on as their importance increased. Who wouldn't? As negotiators or middlemen, they were entrusted to carry on negotiations between the Nigmag and the cousins, and, in these talks, there were always gifts exchanged. Some were fancy talkers with fancy gifts. The *captaine des sauvages* soon learned how to skim the gifts and began to hoard, exchange, or sell these gifts to the highest bidder; big bids too. I thought there might be historical records among the hoarded items, perhaps a lot of them. I recall hearing about one of these stashes. It's a long shot, but a long shot is better than nothing."

Hearing this story made Pallet hopeful he might find more information about the Nigmag if he found one of these stashes. He has learned not to raise his hopes too much, but now, it seemed, he might have a chance to find out more on the history of the Nigmag.

Gionig continued: "With most treasure of this kind, there were guards who took care of it. At the time, they believed there was no greater guard than a sgaatagamootj. These are dead people who have passed on before their time. An untimely death can bring on untimely results. Sometimes they are unusually angry that they drew the short stick and had to leave early. Some of them are just nasty without rhyme or reason. You don't want to be messing with them if you don't have to.

"You may ask how did they entice a sgaatagamootj to guard the treasure? Well, after hiding their treasure, the *captaine des sauvages* drew sticks to see who would be the guard and vow to protect the treasure forever. The short stick was a bad deal; the one who got it lost his life.

"Feeling secure that their treasure trove was protected, the *captaine des sauvages* saw further opportunities that arose during difficult negotiations between the Nigmag and the cousins. As difficulties escalated, the gifts became more elaborate and the *captaine des sauvages* realized the benefits of these protracted talks. They were not above withholding information to lengthen the talks; a delay here, a delay there would be to their benefit. Well, after awhile that's all there was, just constant delay.

"As time moved on and disagreements continued, the treasure troves got larger and they needed places to hide them. With so much treasure, they needed more protection. Then the sgaatagamootj began to put their own hierarchy in place; the number ones had their numbers twos, that sort of thing. The latest guards became extra serious about protecting the stash. Then a change occurred; this change happened quickly because there was so much gain involved. Soon the sgaatagamootj began to hurl objects: twigs and pebbles, and later sticks and stones to keep people away.

These flying objects are dangerous: it's not mosquitoes or butterflies you're batting at. You have to be careful with these objects flying through the air."

After the story, Pallet and Gionig sat quietly near the campfire. Pallet didn't know what to do with the story. From what he has seen so far, he is willing to believe it.

"Interesting, those *captaines*," Pallet muses, still thinking about the story.

"Yes, they are. They're still here. Still at it. They will always be here in one form or another. There are always opportunities to be had," observes Gionig, sipping his tea like a sage.

"Were they a part of Nigmageoeiatotitj the world?" Pallet asks.

Gionig is not sure how to answer but he has to say something. "Could be. You never know what they are up to. They're into everything,"

Pallet stirs his tea and carries on the thought. "The Nigmag wanted relatives throughout the world. And they wanted the knowledge that came with it. There was much knowledge to be gained by marrying outside your village."

"Looks like it turns out that way," Gionig replies.

"Still working on it," says Pallet. "The Nigmag diaspora."

Pallet stokes the fire and gets ready to go fishing. He doesn't have a fishing line or hooks, so he makes a weir at an open place in the frozen river. With a long stick, he moves some rocks on the bottom, and he stirs up the sand that floats down river. After making a big hole on the bottom, he places bigger stones in a circle around the hole with an opening for the water to flow in. He lays spruce boughs across the rocks. The fish enter the weir through the hole and hide in the spruce bough covered weir. Fish are drawn to covered, protected areas. The opening works one way. Once the fish swim in, there is no way out. Later, Pallet comes back, removes the cover, and takes out enough fine trout for an excellent meal.

Before darkness sets in, Pallet and Gionig make preparations for a cold night. They gather firewood and put more spruce boughs on their anapiigan. They cover the cold ground with more boughs. While they do their chores, the trout are slowly cooking, propped up on crossed sticks near the fire. Pallet now puts green cedar on the fire to make smoke that will flavour the fish. Once they are done he sprinkles dried, ground up cranberries over the trout. He brews up another pot of Labrador tea from the leaves he still has in his bag.

Before dark, both settle down inside the anapiigan [leanto] and eat their supper. While they are eating, Gionig suddenly says, "I remember where one of the *captaine des sauvages* made one of their stashes. Big stash too."

"How would you know that?"

"Well, sometimes I don't know how I know what I know. It seems to come and go. Sometimes if there is a need, it comes up. If there is a need, then I can sometimes remember. I can tell you the stash is about a quarter moon travelling from here."

"What will we find there?" asks Pallet,

"Well, you never know with our gathered or stolen things. Maybe secrets. I think it worth a try. I might find some needles to mend my tattered rabbit skin clothes."

"Yes, it's good to have needles."

CHAPTER 12

In the evening, Taapoategl curls into a fetal half moon. She feels safer in this position. Her breath, as it swirls around the inner circle of her body, keeps her warm. She remembers the smell of sleeping family members in their winter oigoôm and the temporary feeling calms her down. In the dark, she is able to think more clearly; there are no distractions. She remembers attending Nigmag otootaen and some of the ceremonies involved in these funerals. She knows the close relatives of the deceased give an oration. With all the ceremonies it could sometimes take several months, or even years, to bury the remains.

Taapoategl recalls that the otootaen can be lengthy because it involves remembering and talking about the deeds of the deceased, their family lines, their favourite food, or their journey through life. It is a structured affair, but not so rigid that new ideas could not be incorporated. All circumstances are different and you must be willing to adapt. Plus, you never know what might happen with the living. People can usually handle their own death better than another's. Regret may set in and people become inconsolable; whatever had happened before the death that causes the regret cannot be changed.

There are many events that surround Nigmag burial. Taapoategl tries to remain focused. She tries to guard against distractions. She has to remain calm. She doesn't have the luxury of time when one can experience the ancient Nigmag ceremony, but she feels it is certainly possible for a burial to be completed. She is the closest family member; she has to prepare and perform the otootaen. Before beginning the oration, Taapoategl thinks of the safe shadows of her past, her pleasant times with her aunt. Her memories lead her to think about herself, which according to the Nigmag is a crucial aspect of the otootaen. You have to deal with yourself, as well as dealing with the remains.

Taapoategl begins the oration by remembering Attaoisoogatiget's life. She remembers, and silently speaks her thoughts. "My auntie had braided a religious trinket in her hair when she converted to the cousins' religion. Even though she had converted, her sacred prayers were saved for Mndoo, the original Nigmag creator, who provided the guidance and protection she needed. Her life with Mndoo was simple; there was no homage or sacrifice. There were bountiful resources and so there was no need to gain from another person's harvesting. She led a good life and did not take from the labour of others. With so many missionaries scouring the bushes for Nigmag converts, she welcomed the attention and displayed generosity, as requested by the missionaries. She made offerings of food and animal pelts to their new god because she thought it was the neighbourly thing to do. She was raised with Nigmag values of generosity, politeness, and neighbourliness."

Although Taapoategl is young, she knows what is happening to the Nigmag. Religion is important in her home and the missionaries were upsetting Nigmag beliefs and ceremonies. She thinks about what she knows. "Mndoo, the Nigmag creator, is either female or male depending on the words used. Both are important. The female creator can't expect more favours than the male creator. Sometimes belief and reality sit on opposite ends of the bench. Good intentions are important for the Nigmag."

Taapoategl falls deeper into what she can remember: "Nigmag beliefs are losing out to the new religion; missionaries count converts as a victory, like in a war. The Nigmag seem to be at the centre of a storm, so much unrest and rapid change. In both Tlaagati and in the spirit world, Mndoo, the Nigmag creator, is more and more disrespected. The missionaries say Mndoo is an evil force and should disappear from all Nigmag prayers and talk. Missionaries make converts to the new religion and denounce Mndoo. Denouncing your religion means that the Nigmag have to denounce themselves and their ancestors and all the stories of their people."

The next day Taapoategl avoids food and water. Two days later, she sits by the brook with memories of her auntie streaming through her mind. She remembers Attaoisoogatiget's claim to fame was the way she quoted the stories and prophecies of her mother, Gitjoo Miidiee Niipi.

It was a time of choice as it was time of no choice. The currency of the beaver pelt had almost disappeared. The cod swam into brine and were carried away over the ocean. As the trees disappeared from cutting and burning, the rivers turned brown, washing away the land. The salmon tried to jump through stone. The caribou made a gallant but fruitless last stand. Fish tried swimming on dry land.

Taapoategl thinks about other rituals she should perform for the burial. Her grandfather had told her the worst change of all is that the Nigmag no longer know where their bellybuttons are buried. She remembers it is the supreme insult to tell a Nigmag they don't know where their bellybutton is buried. The umbilical connection to mother has always been buried in Tlaagati. But now these burial sites are burnt, pillaged, washed away, destroyed. She thinks about how the seeds of the new religion were planted and grew like wildfire, and how, with the cousins' invasion, the land has become a possession instead of a partner.

Memories of her aunt seem to be everywhere for Taapoategl. One story she remembers is about children. Her aunt told about the growing disconnection between children and their parents and relatives: "Gesalogig ag gipalogig" [we love them and we fear them] was one of her famous lines. She told stories about how children would turn against their parents.

Her aunt told a story about a four-year old boy, Elosgatamit, who spat on an elder's face. The insult took place at a major Nigmag gathering, and there was no apparent reason for it. To add to the mystery, the mother and boy disappeared immediately. Later, stories were told of the boy developing lockjaw, and the mother, too, was not able to smile again. These were troubling stories that tended to be forgotten until auntie found an occasion to recount them, and bring up a warning in the minds of her listeners.

As these memories play out, Taapoategl's exhaustion overcomes her. She curls up even tighter and falls into a troubled sleep.

CHAPTER 13

First light is on the horizon; Pallet is a first light person. He wants to see the sunlight first thing in the morning. It sets the tone for his day, and, if he is lucky, he sees the sun in the evening just before it goes over the horizon.

There is a lot to do today. Pallet and Gionig have rested for two days and will take another day to rest. Like old friends, they don't have to talk much. They are comfortable with each other; one has the other's back.

Pallet thinks of a friend he had in his younger years. They had agreed to cover each other backs. They would alert each other if there were any hotspots that needed tending to; douse the fire, that sort of thing. This agreement went well for a while until Pallet heard conflicting news about his friend. It was a bit too late for him by the time he found out his friend was a pyromaniac. Pallet had learned his lesson and moved on.

Pallet knows he should return to the island to retrieve Gionig's supplies and belongings. They both nod and smile without speaking as they look toward the island. There are no signs of activity. Snow fallen during the night now covers all tracks. Both nod again, as if hesitant to speak about what needs to be done. Both have unexpressed misgivings about what will happen if Gionig goes back to the island. He is hesitant to ask Pallet for the favour. Maybe Malsem will be there. Then what? They know they have not broken the terms of Gionig's confinement, so there should be nothing to worry about.

Before Pallet leaves, Gionig gives him some instructions. He tells him to keep his left eye open and his right eye closed; that way Pallet will be able to keep a single focus on his task. Pallet also puts a needle on his cap; you never know what traps Malsem may have set, or what trickery he may be up to. When Pallet reaches the island, he doesn't see Gionig's oigoôm. He sees only the remains of the campfire. Now, where the oigoôm was there is a big pine tree.

Pallet has heard of optical illusions, so he knows enough to deny what he sees and keep focused on reality. He puts his hand on the bark of the tree and it feels warm. He presses his hand further and it passes through the bark. It burns a bit, but he doesn't withdraw his hand. Although nothing looks right, he knows he is in the right place. He pushes his hand forward and his body follows. He slowly enters the tree and looks around. There isn't much there; Gionig has led a spartan life. Pallet hastily grabs the snowshoes, bedding furs, dried food, and several braids of sweetgrass.

He stops to reaffirm his focus and keeps one eye closed. He knows there is nothing to fear in nature, but that in his anxiety, he may see things that are not there. Fortunately, his mind knows the difference, at least so far. To avoid possible confusion, he hurries to leave the island. He moves by dead reckoning because all of his tracks have disappeared; either that, or he just doesn't see them. Either way, Pallet is determined to keep his focus. He keeps his eye on Gionig and heads straight for him. He doesn't stop until he reaches the shore. He doesn't feel tired but he is out of breath and breathing hard. The cold air hurts his lungs.

Gionig is smiling and waiting for Pallet to come ashore. Both are glad that nothing happened.

"You did it."

"Yes, it's in the eyes. Thanks for that."

Both are now ready to leave but they have to wait until Pallet catches his breath.

"Were you worried?"

"A bit, but I trust you."

Before heading out, Pallet burns sweetgrass to ask for guidance and safety for their journey. He thanks the creator for the safety that has brought Gionig and Pallet together at this time and place. He asks for future safety and thanks the creator for granting his requests for the future. They leave without further ceremony or fanfare.

The first three days of travel are uneventful. For Pallet, uneventful is not good because that means there are no problems to deal with. Each evening he burns sweetgrass and reaffirms his gratitude for their safety. He says, "It's good to smell sweetgrass from summer harvest in wintertime; yes, the smell of a Nigmag summer in the winter."

As they enjoy the fragrant odour on the third evening, Pallet tells his story about sweetgrass. He heard the story from his grandfather. He remembers clearly when his grandfather told him this story; it was early summer and the leaves of the poplar shimmered like a thousand paddles going upstream. "You remember what has to be remembered." Pallet begins:

"It was a time of liquid land; the earthquake from Europe had not settled. The visitors were expanding furiously on every side and the open sores of history were enlarging. The fish were largely depleted, the animals did know why they were now so few, the pelts were gone, and open fires were set on ancient forest where the Nigmag lived and raised their families. The scalp bounty was in full effect and war parties of scalp hunters were roaming the landscape hunting down all the Nigmag they could find.

"It was during summer and the Nigmag were digging for clams and fishing to supplement their diet. They lived off the forest most of the time, but needed seafood as well. It was an opportunity to teach the youth the fishing methods of their ancestors. Everyone was aware of the dangers of the bounty hunters and all precautions were taken to avoid them.

"A party of two women and two men were sent to the shore to dig for clams. Another party set weirs near a shallow river that flowed into the ocean. A third party collected sweetgrass. While the fishing parties were at the shore, other family members quietly set up camp in the nearby woods. The six children were told to be quiet and play a silent game of memory with thirteen pairs of small flat stones, each pair having the same design. The stones were scrambled up and placed on the ground with the design side down. The children would pick a stone and then try to match the design. Each matched pair was taken out the game, and play continued until the stones were all picked up. Some children couldn't stop giggling when they matched a set of stones. They were told to be quiet.

"The adults gathered boughs and poles to make anapiigans and oigoôms. Extra dry wood was gathered to avoid a smoky campfire. A young woman in her final term of pregnancy kept watch in a clearing above the campsite. She had a moose call horn made of birchbark and was ready to sound the alarm if there was danger of bounty hunters.

"When the clam diggers returned, there was great activity to prepare a feast of clams. Clean ocean water was gathered in a large birchbark container and placed in a large oôo [bowl]. Hot stones from the fire were placed in the water to cook the clams. The Nigmag loved to cook their clams in ocean water; the natural salt went well with the delicious clams. That evening there were no stories told and the campfire was allowed to burn out. The tide readers sat on the ground and drew plans for their journey tomorrow; they were going to the Rise and Fall Rocks. They would be safe there among the ancient burial sites. Before darkness engulfed the shore, all was ready; the birchbark canoes were repaired, the children were safely sleeping, and the sweetgrass had been braided.

"Unbeknownst to the Nigmag, the scalp hunters were watching them from the nearby woods.

"In the dim light of early morning, the hunters descended quietly on the Nigmag camp. Musket fireballs filled the air like angry hornets seeking their warm targets. Many Nigmag, awakened in terror, fell and lay silent like pebbles on the beach. More hunters and a swarm of musket fireballs met children who ran screaming into the woods. Other children followed the adults as they ran towards the sea, only to be cut down by more musket fire.

"As quickly as one can think and as quickly as god can blink, the Nigmag were silenced. The hunters were now all breathing hard.

Almost regretfully, the stoic hunters gathered with relief in a circle near the shore. They felt they had made the world a better place. This pestilence had been destroyed.

"Now came the next stage of this macabre celebration. With well-sharpened knives in hand, the hunters surgically collected the bloody evidence that would result in a handsome bounty payment. The hunters would be paid five guineas by the European colonial government for each male scalp, and even more for the scalps of women and children. This income from the bounty on Nigmag scalps would enable the cousins to purchase supplies and fend off starvation. The bounty money would also go into establishing farms, shipbuilding, and other businesses.

"Sometimes a scream was yet heard, followed by a loud bang, and then silence. Briefly, there came a cry from the effects of air rushing into new-born lungs, and then again silence. The bounty collection was complete. Amniotic fluid was spattered on a rock protruding from the shoreline. Mutilated bodies were thrown on top of each other, others thrown into the sea, and others left on the shoreline. Like a trophy, an eighth-month stillborn, now also hairless, lay on top of the bodies.

"When news of the slaughter reached Gloositeoisg, the Nigmag goddess of water, her anger grew beyond reason. She cursed the religion that allowed this to happen. She set out in her birch canoe and paddled throughout the shoreline gathering all the blood, skin tissue, and bone fragments she could find. Once her canoe was full, her anger returned again. She began to dig graves with a caribou shovel, which soon wore down. She kept digging with her hands. She dug for one hard winter moon overhead. Her fingers wore away and then her hands decomposed, but she still scratched the ground with bare bones protruding from her arms. She dug until she no longer had arms or bones. After she left, all one could see of the massacre site was the rock monuments that stand on the shoreline of the highest tides of Nigmagaagati.

"Gloositeoisg was not able to gather all the remains, and the sea turned an angry red with Nigmag blood. Espipisgoitg, the highest tides in the Nigmag world, quickly claimed the Nigmag remains as blood, skin tissue, and bones dissipated into the watery grave. The tides carried the slaughter fragments throughout the shoreline. The blood, fluid, and mud quickly mixed with the water as it flowed up into the many tributaries. The muddy mixture moved as if hoping to find its many bellybuttons.

"Most of the blood sediments settled and fertilized the tall grass in the marshes and fields. After the hard winter moons overhead, the area had sparse patches of sweetgrass growing, and by summer it was growing in abundance along the shoreline. To this day, the scent of the sweetgrass migrates through the air on a warm breezy summer day, a sad reminder of lives lost.

"For many years the Nigmag had gathered sweetgrass here as part of their religious ceremony, but since the massacre, they make special spiritual offerings where the rock monuments still stand. Special prayers are offered to the children whose lives were cut short by the bounty hunters. Some of them can still be named: Tapoosiitjig Glôgoejt, Siigoneoio Aasoeg, Gonteetj, Gôptjaaoetj, Lentoogtjiitj, Oôgois, Siisiptjiitj, and Oetjgoet the name for the unborn baby.

"The years moved on, and the Nigmag encountered more changes as Espipisgoitg became dotted with pirated property. Access to the shore became difficult as unfriendly landowners objected to the Nigmag ceremonies happening along the shoreline. In later years things did not get any better. Espipisgoitg became even more inaccessible. The shoreline became more restricted and parks began to spring up. Fees were now charged for people to enter. So the Nigmag had to pay a fee to make religious offerings to the victims of the massacre along Espipisgoitg shoreline.

"Although Nigmag are not always able to visit the ancient burial grounds of the highest tides, the scent of the sweetgrass travels great distances to their communities where ceremonies are held each summer. Ironically, as the cousins hold their summer celebrations, the scent of the sweetgrass covers the open sores of history. Taagô."

When Pallet finishes his grandfather's story, they both stare silently into the campfire for a long time.

CHAPTER 14

On the third day, Taapoategl is still preparing to bury her auntie's remains. She must be careful where to make the burial. It must be a place that will be secure and not disturbed. With so many new grave robbers, it should be in an inconspicuous place to prevent the discovery. Otootaen is important to the Nigmag, and Taapoategl is determined to honour the burial.

She returns to the shed and offers prayers to her aunt's severed remains and to any other Nigmag who suffered a similar death. After praying, she prepares to make a Nigmag lesgiigen, a masgoi coffin. As she gathers bark and spruce root, she is mindful that it is the Nigmag's greatest honour to be buried in masgoi. The Nigmag cannot imagine anything bad happening to the remains after they have been secured inside a masgoi lesgiigen; the coffin is impenetrable.

Taapoategl thinks about the many uses the Nigmag have for masgoi in addition to serving as a burial vessel. She remembers her water container and the masgoi sheets on which Nigmag history is recorded. She thinks about how important a masgoi goiten is for water travel. Many times she has heard that a Nigmag's first love is a goiten. She has seen how a masgoi goiten all ribbed up, root sewn, with curved and pointed ends, and a well-carved paddle brings much joy to the hearts of the Nigmag. The earth moves slower when you are in a goiten. With a goiten, you can travel far and wide, inland on rivers and to island lands in the ocean.

Taapoategl brings her thoughts back to responsibility to the dead. She has learned from Nigmag practice that no gain should be made from death; instead, people should give freely to the dead and their family. Stealing from the dead is unheard of.

In the evening, Taapoategl continues the otootaen ceremony. She mentally recites her aunt's story.

"Attaoisoogatiget's favourite earth harvest was sweetgrass, which she used at religious ceremonies or to bring a time of reflection on one's self and earth. She gathered the sweetgrass in mid-summer along with other Nigmag. She often burned sweetgrass as a reminder of the fragility of the balance of life and as a prayer. She also enjoyed the aroma of sweetgrass braided in her hair.

"Attaoisoogatiget taught that burning and offering sweetgrass is a conduit, an ethereal portal, for bringing balance and harmony within the community. She explained that maintaining this balance and avoiding its loss is often difficult because people have to resist the lure of a negative force. For some people, this negative force is very attractive. For some unknown reason, these people fall into a negative path and are lured down into a bad place within.

"In ancient poôin tradition, Attaoisoogatiget kept a needle woven into her hair. A poôin is a gifted person who has the power to manipulate people or events. The power of a poôin is not always evident. There are many who do not display their power, but know what power they have and choose to use it for personal gain. You do not see these poôin much because they are able to manipulate situations to their advantage without arousing suspicion. Poôin often use their gift to manipulate games of chance, and they usually win. But there are also poôin who help the community and share what they gain.

"Attaoisoogatiget was considered a poôin because she was a history keeper, a knowledge sharer, and a performer of ancient rituals at Nigmag ceremonies. For her, the needle in her hair warded off malignant forces, which may result in sickness or family quarrels and disruption. According to her, the skyward space above the needle, lying horizontal, was protected. She believed that an evil force or negative energy was not able to go underneath a needle.

"Attaoisoogatiget was ever vigilant of these forces, and she kept a close eye on her family. If there was imbalance in family relationships or physical conditions, she made needle tea. When she made it, she was aware of the strict traditionalists who want the tea brewed the same way as the ancestors did. To follow this tradition, she made the tea in her masgoi vessel and put small hot stones in the cup until it boiled. At ritual offerings, she sprinkled the needle tea, but depending on the severity of imbalance, some Nigmag put the tea on their bodies; others preferred to drink the tea. In addition, she had a needle at the entrance of her oigoôm. She felt fully protected with the needle in her hair. As an added precaution, she drank, sprinkled, and put tea on her body at each pilei tepgonset [new moon].

"Attaoisoogatiget often talked about her needle, which had been given to her by her grandmother, Matjôteligen. Her grandmother had been an excellent arrowhead maker who bartered her work. She was known to insist that her arrowheads should take only one life. She cautioned that an arrow gains energy when it takes a life. It then hungers for more of this energy, and should not be used again."

Taapoategl remembers how her aunt enjoyed telling about her grandmother's needle that was made long ago in the time of tjioiisis and tjisiisip, the giant four-legged ones and the large winged ones, now extinct. She said this was a time of caution for the Nigmag. Prey and predator were in abundance. It was not unusual for the Nigmag to be prey for the tjioiisis or tjisiisip. The tjisiisip could spot a Nigmag miles away, swoop in, quickly make the catch, and disappear into the sky. The Nigmag then joked they had to walk with one eye looking up and the other one looking down to be on the alert for predators all around. Matjôteligen told Attaoisoogatiget that the needle was made from oiteneiosamo, the nose horn of a tjioiisis that once roamed Nigmagaagati.

Before Taapoategl falls asleep, she looks again at the needle she has taken from her auntie's hair. She marvels at its size. She is tempted to keep it, but taking from the dead is not her way. She is aware the needle had provided spiritual protection for many of her ancestors.

"Why didn't the needle protect my auntie?"

She thinks maybe it did protect her from acting unnaturally toward others. She will return the needle to her aunt.

CHAPTER 15

"You know it won't be easy when we get there. We'll be dealing with characters we can't see, angry characters, blown-em-up, throw-em-up kinds of characters. So burn your sage and sweetgrass, and whatever else may offer us protection."

Gionig spoke in as warning a tone as he could muster.

"We'll be dealing with some nasty characters."

"And the needles," said Pallet. "It's good to have needles."

"Yes," said Gionig, not absolutely certain, but he has to say yes.

They discuss maneuvers for getting past the guards.

"It's hard to defend yourself against invisible agents. You can't attack or retaliate or hurl compressed energy balls at them. Rocks and insults won't hurt the ghosts at all, but their rocks will hurt us for sure," observes Gionig.

"Some of the greatest battles were won with a simple plan and a simple means, like a diversion," he adds.

"Like a sleeping beaver," Pallet jokingly replies. He tries not to laugh but both realize the irony and laugh out loud.

"Yeah, we don't want any sleeping beavers flying through the air. They have a nasty bite, those critters." Gionig says, trying to add humour to the story.

Then, seriously, he adds, "The guards have things that hurt, and are not afraid to use them."

Gionig adds, "Sometimes you need protection from benevolent forces as well."

"So will there be benevolent forces there? Both can hurt?" Pallet asks, trying to understand. He wants to prepare as well as possible.

"Yes, there is a chance. Most times there is a balance of evil and good," Gionig said as if he had experience in these matters.

"Ok, we'll be ready for the benevolent forces. I assume we will need protection from them; I hope not, but we'll be ready," Pallet replies. Just talking about it gives him greater confidence.

The co-conspirators feel better with what they have discussed. It is a way of reassuring themselves they will be ready for anything hurled their way. They feel good enough to jokingly pigeon-chest themselves as if they are bravely marching into battle with shoulders back and heads held high.

They decide to walk in single file with Pallet in front and Gionig a few paces behind. Each has a needle as a shield or for whatever purpose it may serve. They walk as quietly as possible. Gionig steps directly in Pallet's footprints to avoid making more noise. As they walk towards a valley, Pallet can see a passage with large stones on both sides. A pond lies just beyond the stones. They stop to assess the situation. They don't see any movement or shadows further ahead. It is quiet. This might mean they are close. He tells Gionig what he sees. He nods that he understands. As they advance, Pallet sees leaves moving on the branch of a tree.

"Maybe a squirrel running through or a bird has a nest there," he thinks to himself.

Despite these possibilities, he feels apprehensive and cautious. He points to the branches and Gionig nods. Suddenly, a whistling sound startles them; they both duck. As they had agreed, Gionig looks to the right and Pallet to the left. They make eye contact and silently indicate they haven't seen anything. They hear another whistling noise, like a missile slicing through the air. They know they are in danger. They crawl towards the two stones. And then, there are more missiles flying through the air. First there is a whistle, the sound of a projectile cutting though the leaves, and then the hard thud when it strikes something solid.

Pallet is hit. His left shoulder is gashed and starts to bleed.

This is followed by a fury of rocks flying though the air. Some of them are jagged shards. Gionig and Pallet reach the big stones and hug them for protection. They don't see anyone, just rocks flying through the air. They stay as close as possible to the stones.

Soon, larger rocks come flying, hitting closer and closer. Pallet's shoulder is still bleeding. He's anxious and frightened. He wonders if the needles will work. The rocks are coming fast and furious. Pallet draws the needle from his cap and lifts it toward a large incoming rock. The rock splits and lands at his feet.

He smiles and feels more confident, but not for long. The rocks keep coming. The battle continues. He sees that Gionig is waging a similar battle. He is not holding up to the pressure required to split the flying rocks. Exhaustion is setting in fast. Pallet is losing strength. A rock that didn't get split flies by nicking his ear.

"This is getting too close!"

Struggling up on one knee, and at the same time ducking and weaving to avoid the flying projectiles, Pallet sees the pond.

He thinks, "Maybe, maybe."

He gets Gionig's attention. He is also exhausted. Pallet points to the pond and without further communication they start moving. The pond seems far away but in reality it is only a short distance. They are both upright now holding out their needles in defense. Pallet sees a shadow coming toward him, getting darker and darker, closer and closer. He knows there is no time to look up. He staggers towards the pond. His feet are dragging. His whole body feels like it is dragging. Gionig is having the same difficulty. They grab onto each other.

Pallet grasps Gionig around the shoulders, looks at him, and yells, "Jump... jump!"

The water is cold from the mountain runoff. Once they disappear under the water, the rocks stop flying. Under the water with big eyes and bulging cheeks like a cod, Pallet and Gionig regain their composure.

Both are thinking, "Get me the hell out of here."

Finally, they surface and all is quiet. They stay on the surface long enough to catch their breath. They go underwater again and stay there as long as they can. They surface again to talk about their next move. They agree they don't dare leave the water. They can still see the dust settling from the broken rocks. They check for injuries; other than a few facial cuts and bruised legs where fragments bounced off, and the cut on Pallet's shoulder, they feel fine.

But when they jumped in the pond, Pallet lost his needle. They both start diving, looking for it on the bottom of the pond. They can't see anything. There is too much sediment stirred up to see clearly. Pallet dives several more times without success, but each time he dives, he sees a faint light from the side of the pond. He tells Gionig about it, and they decide to investigate. Gionig says he'll go first. He takes a deep breath and dives. He is gone a long time, too long Pallet thinks.

"Who can hold their breath that long?"

Finally, Gionig comes to the surface. He has found a tunnel that leads to a cave through which the light is shining. They decide to face the challenge of the tunnel rather than face angry ghosts with only one needle. They dive into the murky water and swim towards the light.

It's a long swim and Pallet's lungs are ready to burst. Finally, he breaks water and frantically gasps for air, his heart going thump-thump, thump-thump. The air has no taste but mouthfuls of it sure feels good. With hearts pounding, they swim to edge of the water. They crawl out and sit on the floor of the cave to rest. They cannot see much of anything except for shadowy images on the floor and walls of the cave.

With great relief, and still breathing in heavy gulps of air, they slowly recover. In a little ritual, Pallet counts and moves his fingers one by one. They are all there, they all work, and he can still count.

At the top of the cave they can see the outline of spruce tree branches. In the light and shadows they look like long fingers reaching all the way to the floor of the cave. Pallet doesn't move. He is still regaining his breath and normal heartbeat. He is still startled by what has happened, and, now, by what he is seeing. Finally, breathing easier, they both rise, wobbly at first, but with feet wide apart standing firm on solid ground, they regain their balance. Drawn by the light, they climb the wall toward the top of the cave. They peer out of the entrance and see a forest. They push away the branches and climb out of the opening. Where are they? Everything seems different and uncertain. Pallet makes a great effort to hang on to reality with his sense of time.

"Sometimes," he thinks, "time is all we have."

They return to the cave and see something they hadn't noticed in their eagerness to reach the opening – an irregular, strange looking, dust covered mound. Then they see shapes of objects under the dust and begin to clean it away. Coughing, they work faster, clearing away maybe centuries of dust. No one has been here for a long time! Now they are finding pelts, arrowheads and obsidian blades. There are clay pots, metal pots, metal tools, wampum belts and more stone tools, each one ready to be used. Pallet is especially drawn to the stone tools: knives, axes, and scrapers. He cuts his hand on an obsidian blade when he picks it up. Most of the tools are meticulously decorated with a double curve motif.

Gionig finds rolled up birchbark and tosses it to Pallet who frowns and tells him to be more careful. Pallet puts the bark into the water and slowly unfolds it. Each word jumps out after centuries of incubation. One bark has a list of names, maybe a census; another has a map, perhaps a map of another treasure trove or of boundary lines; another has writing on it. After a quick perusal, Pallet sees that it is a story or a poem.

Gionig finds needles, some bone, some wood, and some metal; they are wrapped in leather. He clutches them in his hand and tells Pallet what he has found. Pallet tells him to keep them safe. They decide to take a minimum of items.

"Not much sense in taking a load you can't carry," says Pallet.

He picks out some birchbark, a few needles, and a stone arrowhead. Gionig says he is not allowed to take anything, but he can carry the knowledge of what they found. Pallet understands; immortals live by their own rules. He offers sweetgrass, some dried food, and a prayer of thanks as a gift to the collection of ancient Nigmag goods. Briefly, they consider spending the night there. They are under cover and warm enough.

Then Pallet reconsiders and says, "That might be risky. Who knows who else is here? There's no sense inviting more danger."

They crawl out of the cave, uncertain which way to go; they didn't want to face the missile fight again. It's late, so they have to find shelter fast. They find a good campsite on the bank of a nearby river. Gionig prepares a fire while Pallet makes an anapiigan and gathers spruce bows for bedding. Soon the campfire is the only light they have.

Pallet begins to talk about *captaine des sauvages*.

"It was the Nigmag plan to Nigmageoeiatotitj the world by having as many relatives as possible, but this did not work out. The *captaines* had their own interests. Their road to freedom was by hook or crook and political power.

Pallet paused and then added; "*The captaines* are still prevalent in Nigmag society. Smart bunch they are; they proceed with their own political agenda."

"Stealth and numbers decide political power," Gionig offered. "You have to have a way with politics and know how to drive the force behind it."

"Nigmageoeiatotitj the world has been around a long time. I remember a story about Piampit," Pallet replies and launches into the story.

"Well, someone who tried to Nigmageoeiatotitj the world was Piampit; his stories and poems are often heard around campfires and at powwows. He had gone to Europe in the earlier years.

He had thought he was a guest, but he later found out he had been coerced onto a ship and was to be sold as a slave in Europe. Being an independent character, he was not acquainted with slavery; he did not make a good slave; he did just what he wanted to do. He was an orator and enjoyed pointing out his battle scars, his shells, and adornments that were signs of accomplishment.

"He spoke several trade languages in his homeland, so it was not surprising he was soon conversing with his captors. He had a storyteller's ego, and demanded attention as he told his stories, interesting at first but eventually annoying. He liked to exaggerate his speech with hand gestures, perhaps a reflection of the sign language he had learned from the old timers. When he got excited telling his stories, his hands were busier than a baseball catcher making crotch signs to the pitcher, a story with a curve or one with a straight knuckleball. His hands were everywhere like magic wands in a circus as the audience stares with riveted attention.

"Touching his heart, he said he was the greatest living poet in Tlaagati and now in Europe. Pointing to his medicine bag around his neck, he said he was a medicine man. Piampit told his audience he was a religious leader in his homeland, that he was considered the man to see when questions arose about religion. He said he was a great hunter. Revealing a scar on his knee, he said it was the result of his battle with two bears. On the day he received the bloody wound, two bears lay dead at his feet. Touching a tattoo on his left hand, he said he was an artist. And when the occasion presented itself, he let the women of the court know he was the greatest lover ever.

"He was always changing, and he encouraged the noble savage image. He always had company in the evening. The ladies of the court were very interested in what this savage had to offer and many returned for repeated offerings. For Piampit, this worked well with his philosophy of Nigmageoeiato the world. Needless to say, his captors decided to return him to Tlaagati. Later, some of his offspring came from Europe to Tlaagati, looking for Pimapit and their Nigmag family. Many stayed with Piampit and learned his ways; some went back to Europe, but became disillusioned and returned to Tlaagati.

"Nigmageoeiatotitj took another form. The Nigmag loved babies and were amazed that the cousins would leave their babies at their oigoôm entrance. It was common practice among the Europeans to abandon the newborns at the doorstep of some Nigmag oigoôm, summer or winter. Some years later, the parents would return and were allowed to take their children, but the children always returned to live with the Nigmag."

In the cold winter night, Pallet was in a talkative mood. He was happy to be alive after the battle they had with the sgaatagamootj [ghosts]. There were moments when Pallet thought they wouldn't make it out alive, but they did.

"Must have been the benevolent forces," he mused aloud.

Pallet continues in his story telling mood. He remembers one of Piampit's poems he has often heard from the old men when they gather to tell stories. He has heard it so often he can recite it by heart.

Etlapegatog	He is swinging it
Etlintog	He is singing
Etlapegatog	He is swinging it
Etlintog	He is singing
Amnepegatog	He is swinging it all around
Etlintog	He is singing
Amnepegatog	He is swinging it all around
Amniintog	He is singing all around
Teoapegatog	He swings it and throws it out
Etlintog	He is singing
Teoapegatog	He swings it and throws it out
Teointog	He is singing while he goes outside
Pisgopegaato	He swings it and throws it inside
Pisgointog	He sings as he enters
Pisgopegaato	He swings it and throws it inside
Pisgointog	He sings as he enters

Sesapegaatog	He swings it in a scattering motion
Elintog	He is singing
Sesapegaatog	He swings it in a scattering motion
Seesintog	He is singing in his song and spreads all around
Sesapegaatog	He swings it in a scattering motion
Elintog	He is singing
Sesapegaatog	He swings it in a scattering motion
Egigaalintog	He is singing away from it
Oentagaapegaatog	He swings it quietly
Oentagpit	He sits quietly
Oentagaapegaatog	He swings it quietly
Oentagteg	It is quiet
Oentagaapegaatog	He swings it quietly
Oentagpit	He sits quietly
Oentagaapegaatog	He swings it quietly
Oentagpit	He sits quietly
Gootjeotosit	He crosses himself
Oentagpit	He sits quietly
Gootjeotosit	He crosses himself
Oentagpit.	He sits quietly
Geepistanenat	His hearing is impaired
Ag neemiteeget	And he can see
Geepistanenat	He hearing is impaired
Ag neemiteeget	And he can see
Nemiatl	He sees him
Pemssinag	As he flies by
Nemiatl	He sees him
Pemssinag	As he flies by

Ginisgositat	The sharp nail footed
Anseleoit	Angel
Ginisgositat	The sharp nail footed
Anseleoit	Angel
Osomoitginisgasitat	The horned and sharp nail footed
Anseleoit	Angel
Osomoitginisgasitat	The horned and sharp nail footed
Anseleoit	Angel
Gooltjetosit	He crosses himself
Gooltjetaal	He crosses it
Gooltjetosit	He crosses himself
Gooltjetaal	He crosses it

Gionig laughs as Pallet finishes the poem and says. "The old Nigmag said that Piampit was a bit old fashioned about some things. He liked to do things the traditional way, or at least his version of traditional. They called him Ole Pussin. I'm not sure what that means, but I've heard he was full of passion and compassion for life."

"Yes, he was," Pallet replies. "Although I don't know what position he had about religion. I think he must have gone beyond or behind it, and just enjoyed life. Ole Pussin was old fashioned and had a passion for life. He had it all, if you ask me."

"Piampit. Piampit. Strange name," Gionig mused. "Must mean someone who gets in the way, or who gets there first, or even opportunistic. I like his work and his name matches him well. Ole Pussin, Ole Pussin."

"Maybe he was a distant relative. Hard to say these days," Pallet says as he lies down to sleep. "Don't forget to cross yourself before you go to sleep."

"Can't cross myself. I'm too happy now," replies Gionig and pretends to snore right away.

Before they fall asleep, Pallet remembers a quote from Piampit; "The sin of love is regret. Regret is the sin of love, so sin for love, and love for sin. The sinner comes early and stays to make supper." He doesn't understand the entire saying, but it's one he often remembers.

Pallet and Gionig fall asleep, tired out from a hard day.

CHAPTER 16

Outside the cabin, Taapoategl begins her day by offering a single prayer. She doesn't have sweetgrass to offer, but this won't make any difference because the creator will still hear her prayers. She prays that her captors will let her go. She prays for her safe return to her family. She prays that she will know what to do with her aunt's remains. At this point, prayer is all she has.

It's a comfort to be outdoors. She breathes the cool air; at least she can do this freely. She walks to the edge of the woods and begins to collect sticks to make a small sacred scaffold for the otootaen. She knows that whenever possible, the Nigmag place the remains of a deceased person on a scaffold for the duration of the burial ceremony. The remains are enclosed in a lesgiigen made of birchbark and sown shut with spruce roots. Often, the remains are placed in a position earlier requested by the deceased. Other instructions, as given, are also followed.

She remembers that depending on circumstance, the remains may be stored in the lesgiigen for a year or more. The period of time depends on the deceased's request. Some give instructions to be buried in the spring when new growth comes to Tlaagati. The final resting place may take time to complete if the request is to be buried near family members or friends at a distant place.

Respect now overcomes the odour of the scalp for Taapoategl. She hides it under her cloak and takes it to the brook. Keeping it out of sight of the cabin, she scrubs the inside of the scalp with sand. She takes a sharp flat stone and carefully cleans away the soft tissue making sure not to cut or damage the scalp. She is not sure why she is cleaning it, but the Nigmag insist on keeping clean so it makes sense to clean her aunt's remains.

"Something about personal pride," she thinks.

She puts the scalp out of sight on a tree branch to dry. She mixes sand with the scraped tissue and places it on a flat rock to dry. In the cleaning ritual, Taapoategl has introduced the sacred laapaltineoie [water process] to the otootaen, which is crucial because of its cleansing and nourishing quality.

Later, after the scalp and tissue have begun to dry, she carefully places them in a cone of bark. She temporarily ties the lesgiigen closed with spruce roots. She doesn't know all the burial ceremonies, but she knows there are gifts to be offered to her aunt. At this point, her love for her aunt dictates what she does. Even though Taapoategl thinks about what she is going to do, it is different when she actually comes to do it. This part of the ceremony is quiet; all thoughts and prayers remain quiet. She acts with silent respect. It is a secret silence. The only sound is the brook flowing by.

The ceremony helps her move with the present. Each thing she does is new to her. She doesn't know what to do with the lesgiigen at this stage. She only knows she has to hide it, so she hides it near the woodpile. She is the only one who goes there. The woodpile is not the scaffold she has hoped for, but it will do for now.

Afterwards, she sits by the brook with no particular thoughts in mind. She feels good that she has begun the process. The smell of her hands reminds her of what she has done. She washes her hands by rubbing sand on them to help clean away the smell. The smell still lingers. She bursts two bubbles of gum from a fir tree. The strong scent of the tree overcomes all other smells. Taapoategl reminds herself to include fir pitch as one of the gifts. From now on, each time she smells fir gum she will remember what she did today.

She realizes it has been four days since she found her aunt's remains. The time has flown by like clouds on a windy summer day. It seems only moments ago that she was struggling in the shed. She now sits in silence in the dark cellar and continues her otootaen oration.

Taapoategl remembers how Oasteo and Attaoisoogatiget had always been willing to share Nigmag history with her. They knew children needed a path to stand on, a path that will help them discover what is new, to look ahead and see if the future is bringing something new or not, and if so, why, and if not, why not. In addition to knowing the path, the sisters wanted her to learn writing so she could exchange ideas, instruction, religion, knowledge of the forest, of the plants and animals, of survival and of the whole Nigmag way of life. Both of them were more than happy to help teach her how to write.

She was five-winter moons overhead when she began to learn gômgoetjoigassigel. Earlier, she played with other children who were making marks on the sand. One of the children drew a deer and wrote that her uncle harvested it. Another child drew fish and wrote how much he liked to eat fish. The children liked to leave messages on the sand. People were careful to not walk on the messages. The younger children wondered why the messages were always gone in the morning and there was a fresh surface to write on. They were told the tide came and took their message away; so if they wanted to write to a family member, the tide would deliver the message.

Taapoategl remembers how her mother and aunt instilled a sense of pride and necessity in her for the ancient Nigmag writing. She honed her proficiency in writing and reading by making notes on birchbark to her mother and aunt. She wrote about the events of the day: someone dried fish, someone hauled firewood, someone brought stones for the sweat lodge, or someone made ice sticks. Most of the notes were short, the kind that busy children make, always in a hurry to enjoy the next moment.

Among the many stories the sisters told, they had a soft spot for their great uncle, Pogseteo who, like the sisters, had a flair for theater. They liked describing how his hands became animated the minute there was an audience. It didn't take much of an occasion or persuasion for him to put on a performance. The sisters recounted how Pogseteo staged a play at Port Royal that included cousins from across the ocean. The performance was falsely recorded in the cousins' records as the first European theatre in the land of the Nigmag.

The sisters told her that staging great entertainments was a family tradition with Pogseteo. He had a niece who was in charge of organizing Nigmag winter celebrations with music, dance, and singing, and always plenty of food. The Nigmag helped the cousins survive their first winter. The cousins joined the Nigmag celebrations and called them "winter's cheer."

The two sisters had a flair for theater like their great uncle. They regaled her with stories about tjioiisis and tjisiisip, and the time when large birds and animals shared the world with the Nigmag. During the days of tjioiisis, the Nigmag were small people next to the large animals. The Nigmag moved quickly and watchfully in under the trees, avoiding the open fields and open water. They had to be alert to avoid becoming part of a tjioiisis meal. Those large claws and teeth could deliver a deadly blow without warning.

Taapoategl remembers how, during gatherings, the two sisters would not miss a chance to do some theatre about the historic birds and animals. The sisters had a performance about an encounter between a Nigmag and a tjisiisip, the giant bird that would silently fly from the mountaintop to snatch up a Nigmag. Attaoisoogatiget flapped her arms wildly like the wings of a giant bird, and her sister would scream and scamper into the under brush for safety. Attaoisoogatiget would land looking confused and would recite her part of the play:

Tami Aamen

Nigmag, Nigmag, tami aamen?
Nigmag, Nigmag, where are you?
Nigmag, Nigmag, tami aamen?
Nigmag, Nigmag, where are you?
Aamen? Aamen? Tami aamen?
Are you here? Are you here? Where are you?

Nigmag, Nigmag, tami elien?
Nigmag, Nigmag, where do you go?

Nigmag, Nigmag, tami elien?
Nigmag, Nigmag, where do you go?
Elien. Elien. Tami elien?
You go. You go. Where do you go?

Nigmaagtjiitj, Nigmaagtjiitj, atoaoigasin.
Little Nigmag, you know how to hide.
Nigmaagtjiitj, Nigmaagtjiitj, atoaoigasin.
Little Nigmag, you know how to hide.
Atoaoigasin, atoaoigasin.
You know how to hide. You know how to hide.

Tjinemtjitj, oeetjoltes. Oeetjooltes.
Little man, I will find you. I will find you.
Eepittjitj, oeetjoltes. Oeetjooltes.
Little woman, I will find you. I will find you.
Oeetjoltes. Oeetjooltes.
I will find you. I will find of you.

Nigmaagtjiitj, tjinemtjitj, eepittjitj
Little Nigmag, little man, little woman,
Oeetjooltogsep. Oeetjooltogsep.
I will find you all. I will find you all.

Nigmaagtjiitj, tjinemtjitj, eepittjitj,
Little Nigmag, little man, little woman,
Maagisigasooltioôg. Maagisigasooltioôg.
All of you cannot hide. All of you cannot hide.

Nigmag, Nigmag, tami elien?
Nigmag, Nigmag, where are you?
Nigmag, Nigmag, tami elien?
Nigmag, Nigmag, where have you gone?
Tami aamen? Tami aamen? Tami elien? Tami elien?

Where are you? Where are you? Where have you gone?
Where have you gone?

Nigmaagtjiitj, Nigmaagtjiitj maagisigasioen. Maagisigasioen.
Maagisigasioen.
Little Nigmag, little Nigmag, you cannot hide. You cannot
hide. You cannot hide.
Nigmaagtjiitj, Nigmaagtjiitj maagisigasioen. Maagisigasioen.
Maagisigasioen.
Little Nigmag, little Nigmag, you cannot hide. You cannot
hide. You cannot hide.

Nigmaagtjiitj, Nigmaagtjiitj, oaenteoaasin, oaenteoaasin,
oaenteoaasin.
Little Nigmag, little Nigmag, You are a skeleton. You are a
skeleton. You are a skeleton.

Her aunt would hop around like an overgrown raven and make enough noise to scare any Nigmag who may have been close by. As she hopped across the ground, dust would fly and create cover for the Nigmag. If the Nigmag was to make a run for it, this was the time; just disappear in the dust and don't look back. The giant bird, frustrated and angry about losing its prey, flapped its wings wildly and flew off as hungry as before.

While the dust was settling, her mother was coughing. She couldn't be seen for all the dust. It was difficult to see which bush she was hiding under. As the dust settled, a large brown rock began to move. To the astonishment of the audience, the rock first rose in the middle then it seemed to be crawling away, moving with a circular motion.

Someone yelled out, "Geeooget! [earthquake] The earth is moving! The world is coming to an end! Gather your family and get ready!"

The brown rock began to rise like a mountain and kept growing until it was taller than any Nigmag in the audience. Then the mountain began to shrink until it was flat on the ground again.

Everything was back to what it was; all was safe. Then her mother coughed again, as if to begin the earthquake again. But this time, she sticks her hand out from under the rock, which turns out to be a large moose hide. Her mother crawled out, stood on top of the moose hide, and she recited these words:

Siisip, Siisip,
Bird, bird,
Geettjool nestooan.
I know you are smart.

Siisip, Siisip,
Bird, bird,
Geettjool pagsigpamalaan.
I know you are absolutely lazy.

Siisip, Siisip,
Bird, bird,
Geettjool getoo gelnin.
I know you want to hold me.

Siisip, Siisip,
Bird, Bird,
Getoo ooigpin.
You yearn to enjoy eating me.

Siisip, Siisip,
Bird, bird,
Getoo maagoomin.
You want to eat me.

Siisip, Siisip,
Bird, Bird,
Negee getoo tjigpin.
Now, you want to finish eating me.

Siisip, Siisip,
Bird, bird,
Gettjool pagsigpamalaan.
I know you are absolutely lazy.

Siisip, Siisip,
Bird, Bird,
Gettjool gaaoisiin.
You are hungry.

Siisip, Siisip,
Bird, Bird,
Gagi telaasin. Gagi telaasin. Gagi telaasin.
You did it to yourself. You did it to yourself. You did it to yourself.
Ôaati…
Well now…

Taapoategl remembers that after this small play the sisters and the audience all broke into great laughter. It was difficult to say if the audience or the sisters enjoyed the play more. They loved to perform. Like good actors, both made notes about their performances. Some lines did not go over as well as they would have liked; maybe use different lines next time, or shorten this or that part.

She recalls how the sisters taught her everything they could about Nigmag writing. Even though she and her family could already communicate with writing on birchbark, the process of Nigmag writing was not settled.

Gômgoetjoigasigel had a difficult beginning. It was about survival and relaying information by writing. During their travels and harvests, the Nigmag would leave information about their activity, information as to where or when the salmon were running, or which route was the most direct or safest. The flat rock drawings were excellent for relaying information, but flat rocks were not always available. To address the issue, the elders called a gathering of the Nigmag to discuss the best ways to relay information efficiently.

The sisters related how up until then, the message runners relayed information about meetings, burials, and so on. Day runners ran during the day, and the night runners ran at night. Some times the runners could not coordinate their meeting times, so some villages did not get important news like migrating caribou or when the smelts were running. The Nigmag needed a written communication for the runners to deliver to other villages and to hand off to other runners, or for leaving messages for other runners to pick up. Several winter moons had passed overhead, and the Nigmag could not agree. Some Nigmag were using clamshells or leather to write messages or agreements between different families. More importantly, some used wampum, made from clamshell, to clarify these agreements.

At one of the summer Nigmag meetings, a group of young people went night-fishing. They did this type of fishing with a spear and light. Pitchwood was used for the fire, which was placed in the front of the canoe so it shone on the water and the fish could be spotted. A night of fishing could result in enough food to feed all the people at a gathering.

In the early part of the evening or in the early morning, the fishers would see markings left on the river bottom by the gômgoetj, the sucker fish, that were bottom feeders. The gômgoetj scoured the river bottom with their large mouths for worms and insects. The movements of their mouths and fins would leave filigree marks on the bottom. The fishers saw that some of their Nigmag writings resembled the markings left by these fish. This observation was mentioned to the elders and they decided to begin calling the Nigmag writing "gômgoetjoigasigel" [written in the manner of a sucker fish].

Oasteo and Attaoisoogatiget went into great detail about the Nigmag language. Taapoategl remembers their instructions about "tleiaoig," [belonging-to], a word full of feeling that describes the connection between the Nigmag and everything around them. Mother and Auntie used the gômgoetj as an example of this connection. They said to pronounce the word gômgoetj you needed to shape your mouth like the fish looking for food, forming a circle with protruding lips to pronounce "gôm." This is similar to the fish blowing out and causing the food particles to move on the river bottom. Then comes the pronunciation of "m" in which the mouth is closed, like the fish closing its mouth to capture food. The "go" sound requires another mouth protrusion, accompanied by exhaling, and getting set to deliver the final "etj" which comes with a kind of spitting motion indicating the message is complete.

This is the way the sisters explained the connection between the Nigmag and the world around them. They told Taapoategl that the Nigmag language comes from imitating the sounds and motions in nature, the calls of birds or the manner in which a fish gathers food.

They told her about Nigmag who tended to view writing their language on the lighter side. Some Nigmag had a growling style of writing, which was difficult to understand. It looked like an angry style of writing. This made sense because the treatment of the Nigmag by the cousins gave plenty to be angry about. But this was not actually the case. The growling style only meant they were hungry when they wrote the message, so their stomachs were growling. Writing hungry and writing in a hurry made the meaning of their writing hard to understand. If there were mixed up messages, they would be explained as being like a feeding frenzy when the gômgoetj left many undistinguishable marks at the bottom of the river.

Taapoategl had been quick to learn gômgoetjoigasigel. She was a natural learner and was taught to always share what she learned. She remembered that when you shared what you learned, you always learned more about what you know, and others will then also be willing to share. The more you shared, the more you learned. She had practiced her writing by writing on her hand with her fingers. Sometimes she would practice when she was waiting for someone. She liked to make good use of her time.

She and a close friend liked to write on the clouds, sending them on their way to deliver their messages. There were always return messages but you had to figure out what they meant. This was difficult because the messages came back as figures. They would see a bear, a human face, or fish in the sky. If you wrote to someone who had a fish name and you saw a fish in the sky that meant they had received the message. Taapoategl was always glad when her aunt, whose name was Trout, got her message.

Sometimes when running along the beach, she would carry a stick and leave a message as she ran. These messages were not always understandable, but she enjoyed the game.

Birchbark was used to carry more urgent messages because the runner could easily carry it and hand it off to the intended receivers or other runners. The masgoi was compact, light, easy to carry and pass on. Nigmag leaders enjoyed writing their instructions on birchbark. The more they wrote messages and exchanged them, the more people gained knowledge.

She remembers when the two sisters showed her the best tools for writing and she had learned to skillfully use them. The perfect tools for writing were a sharp stone or a pointed bone. Some writers preferred a small stick with the end burnt to a point. In the end, it didn't matter what a person wrote their message with, it was just good hearing news about their activities.

Taapoategl preferred to use a sharp stone to write her messages; it was easy to carry a stone in her pocket. She wrapped her writing stone in leather to protect the sharp edge. Now, she will use it to write messages and draw Nigmag designs on her aunt's lesgiigen. She will write where and when she was buried. These are small details, but she feels it is important to record them.

Taapoategl rouses from all these memories of her family and community. She stirs and sees the dark cellar with bars of light shining through the door. She gets up and automatically clicks her heels. She has not done this for a long time. She used to watch her grandfather click his heels each time he stood up. It felt good to click her heels like her grandfather.

CHAPTER 17

In the morning, Pallet and Gionig are not greatly surprised to see it is suddenly winter again. Time has become unpredictable. In addition, they find a birchbark bowl the size of an ocean-going canoe sitting near a roaring fire. The bowl is full of food: venison, tea, fish, maple sap, moose butter, and fowl. Another container is full of berries and nuts. It is a sight that makes them wonder if they had died and gone to heaven.

Still sleepy-headed, still finding their eyes, they didn't believe what they were seeing. What a meal! No expense has been spared in preparing this meal; a very fine meal indeed, a meal fit for poôin, sagamao, ginap, and malpalaiet.

Without thinking, Pallet puts his hand on his stomach in preparation for a feast. His eyes are as big as crab apples, his nostrils like two full moons taking in the sight and smell of such food.

"I see something from the ground; I see something from the air; I see something from the river. Only good food can smell so good. Ah... we'll be eating from the land, sky, and water this morning."

Pallet added with humour, "And if we run out, we still have some nuts and berries and rabbits."

Gionig looks beyond his nostrils and stomach for tracks.

"Who brought this food?" Pallet asks. "Why? What's the explanation? There are no tracks to be seen; there are no signs, just this food."

"It's Malsem," Gionig snaps uncharacteristically. "He knows I'm off the island, and he wants to let me know he knows, that sorry weasel."

Gionig is worried. Momentarily, he thinks about returning to the island, but no, he didn't break any conditions in leaving the island. He feels safe but still unsettled.

"Don't worry," Gionig says. "He usually doesn't bother with mortals... not much a challenge, I guess. Although drowning to leave the island, now that was pretty damn smart. He may be stinging a bit from that; a big sting up his ass, as far as I'm concerned. He thought he would have me there forever. Haa... forever always comes to an end. Forever... you fool. Anyway, I think we're safe; we didn't break any rules when I left the island. You didn't break any rules either. But he wants to let us know that he knows. So don't worry. He's just pissed off that I'm off the island. His problem. We don't have to worry. If he could have, he would've sent us back to the island by now. Not to worry. We don't need his food."

Pallet has not moved from his sitting position. He is salivating like a spittlebug in mating season. He is frozen; he doesn't know what to do. This is a new experience. With all that food in front of them, Pallet is disorientated. He just sits, half smiling, but he can't move.

"Why not accept this gift?" he muses. "It's rude to not accept a gift. So what if someone knows where we are. No big deal. There's a lot of space here, even for those with big issues."

Pallet has difficulty understanding Gionig. He doesn't want to understand. All he can understand now is that there is a great meal in front of him and he wants to get his hands on it.

Gionig stokes the roaring fire and with a long stick slowly pushes all the food into the fire. He breaks the stick on his knee and throws it into the fire. Both the food and the stick make a sizzle, a hiss, and a puff. Smoke rises from the fire.

Gionig, like the final judgment has come, says, "I don't eat food from an old friend who offers new food to an old friend. Even if he has moose butter, I won't touch it."

Pallet is bewildered but doesn't say a word. He stands up and walks around. He stops and stands like totem pole, eyes straight ahead, hands to his sides, wings tucked in, feet planted firmly on the ground. Then he goes to his pack basket and gets out a little dried meat and a few berries. They quietly eat their meager provisions.

Finally, Pallet says, "So what now... where to now?"

Gionig, somewhat nervously, says, "Well, we are in the right place. I'm here, you're here, and Malsem is not here. We interact here but not there. We're safe."

Gionig sounds determined but not confident.

"There? Where is there?" Pallet asks blankly still trying to recover from what had just happened.

"Where you found me," Gionig says knowingly. "Where we are going is the right place to be. We're in the right place. Wouldn't want to be anywhere else."

The rest of the day is spent in contemplation. They are both quiet. Pallet sets a few snares. Gionig repairs the snowshoes.

The next morning is cold. The two companions move briskly about. As if to conserve energy, they don't talk much. They eat from their dried food supply and make Labrador tea to warm up. They talk about what to do next.

Gionig suggests they go see Sogoi, the auntie; "I'm sure she'll have some stories about the Nigmag. She lives some way from here, but we can rest when we get there. She comes from a family of orators. She has a lot to say. She'll be happy to have company. Of course, she'll want to hear stories about our travels and she'll have stories as well. It will be a good rest, and it will give us time to think about where to go next. We have to move fast now, I can see a snowstorm in those clouds."

They prepare their backpacks, their snowshoes, and other supplies. Pallet removes his snares and picks up the rabbit he has caught for their next meal. He tells Gionig they should stop early tonight, so he can set some traps to get some fresh game.

After three days, Pallet and Gionig come to a large lake with a cabin on the east end. Before crossing the lake, they announce their arrival with a "Goee." They do this several times before they reach the cabin. They are greeted at the door and invited in. Sogoi recognizes Gionig and asks him how he got off the island. He nods and makes a motion toward Pallet.

"How did you get him off the island?" Sogoi asks.

"Oh, I had to drown him and revive him after," Pallet replies, sounding almost comical.

"Did you smoke him back to life?"

"That was the only way to bring him back after I got him off the island. I don't think he wanted to leave. But he saw a chance and he took it. I'm glad he did."

Sogoi had a pot of stew cooking near the fireplace. She hands each visitor a bark plate, and they quickly and noisily devour their food. No one talks while they eat.

After the evening meal, Pallet tells Sogoi his story, his quest, and his search for the Nigmag. He asks her if she knows anything about gômgoetjoigasigel written on the birchbark. He hands her the bark he found at the treasure trove. She looks at the list and then looks at Pallet.

"I don't know all the names, but it looks like names I heard before when old Nigmag were offering prayers for loved ones who had passed. The map, I'm not sure, but I think it's an ancient code for a Nigmag burial site. Off hand, the only one I can think of who might know is Malsem, but you already know who he is."

"Do you know where he is?" Pallet asks, sounding more eager than he felt. He had heard so much about Malsem he wasn't sure he wanted to meet him.

"I am not sure," Sogoi said speaking thoughtfully. "The gods and demigods like the north. They like cold and pristine, I guess."

Pallet says no more. He doesn't want to seem anxious to travel further north.

Sogoi suddenly asks, "Did you find any booze in the trove?"

Surprised by the question, Pallet replies, "There were some empty bottles there." With a wink, he adds, "I guess the guards had a little nip."

Sogoi agrees, "Yup, ghost, gods, and booze. That's quite the trinity. Well I'm not sure about ghosts but gods and booze, now that's whole different kettle of fish. Sit down and I'll tell you a story. I heard this story from my aunt, who lived to well past one hundred. Her long life and memory were appreciated and respected by the Nigmag. Even in old age, she would still set traps within a half a day walk around the camp. Only elders and young people were allowed to set traps within this perimeter. This was the Nigmag way to keep the elders independent. The elders also contributed the stories they had heard. People looked forward to hearing their stories. It didn't matter that the stories were told over and over again. Auntie particularly liked the one about god and booze.

"In the early colonizer days, the European missionaries, the spiritual colonizers, were in a religious frenzy because the land of the Nigmag was crawling with potential religious converts. But Nigmag religion and philosophy was already well established so converting them would take much effort and maneuvering. But the missionaries had a god driven goal to redeem the Nigmag by hook or by crook or by god, and they had a demonic ally.

"The colonizers, in the name of civilization and Christianity, were also in a frenzy over the Nigmag land and resources. The colonizers were primed for exploitation, which meant they saw the land as belonging to them to do with whatever they wanted. They had no feeling of belonging to the land. They had no sense of a reciprocal relationship between land and humans. The colonizers ignored the reality of the Nigmag's sanguine and reciprocal tie to the land and the fact that this tie to the land was at the centre of Nigmag religion.

"For the Nigmag, there was already a religious hierarchy about the connection to the earth and creation, and understanding this connection often meant surrendering to the Gisoolg, the Nigmag creator, by various means. You had to be careful because of the spiritual proximity between earth and creator. The Nigmag used religion to coalesce the two. Religion could be tricky. If it had too many restrictions, it could stultify a person and obstruct a meaningful life. Despite this danger, the Nigmag felt there was a need to experience the two realms, and performed activities and ceremonies to connect the two.

"Earth bound mentality was the main obstacle, and some, but not all, Nigmag had the ability to enter a hypersensitive state by not eating for several days or by entering a steam temple to perform a water cleansing ceremony. The ceremony was magnified when you entered the temple after a five day fast.

"The domed steam temple, large enough to hold ten people, was usually framed up with young saplings and covered with animal hides. Inside, the centre had a hole in the ground where heated stones from a sacred fire nearby were placed and sprinkled with spring water to make steam.

"Entering the temple was a symbolic ingress into the mother's womb where you were surrounded by warm spiritual vapour. You had to enter backward, feet first. In the dark of the steaming temple, every sound is heard, every breeze felt, and every mental deviation a possible disaster because you had to keep a dead centre focus on the purpose of the ceremony. It could be a dangerous experience. To avoid disaster, the Nigmag lowered their heart rate and counted their heartbeats. With intent and intensity, they were able to complete the symbolic connection between the creator and earth. Not all were expected to reach this state or readily surrender to the god experience. It was not long before the Europeans called this state a religious stupor.

"The colonizers could not fully understand the dome temple experience and sought enlightenment by entering the ceremonies. Their participation often resulted in more of a physical cleansing than religious experience. The colonizer, however, had brought with them another means for reaching a religious stupor, another way to reach their god. They brought a vehicle that would ensure a spontaneous religious stupor. They said it was the magical symbolic blood of the savior. This new tool for entering a religious stupor required no preparation, which removed individual responsibility for the event. Now, anyone could be in a religious stupor and not be responsible for their actions. This seemed strange to the Nigmag, who were always very aware of being responsible for their individual actions.

"This vehicle led to misuse and the Nigmag were demonized as people who could not tame this new tool or hold their use of it in check. For the Nigmag entering the stupor without responsibility was a chaotic religious breakdown, a spiral that lead to a mindless stupor. The colonizers' vehicle for religious stupor did not create a connection between the creator and earth; it did not require preparation or individual responsibility. It wasn't long before taking alcohol became an easy and casual way of religious stupor. Taagô"

Pallet doesn't know what to think of Sogoi's story. He has always enjoyed life and tried to walk carefully over the earth. He believes in unseen forces, which is a help for understanding creation. He feels he understands the state he has to be in to address the creator. But then, if the creator's work were done, why would you have to contact her again. This is Pallet's way of dealing with issues he doesn't totally understand or want to understand.

The three friends turn in for the night. Quietly and still disturbed, Pallet tries to understand Sogoi's story.

"Perhaps a good rest will give me a better grasp of what I have heard," he thinks as he drifts into sleep.

When Pallet wakes up, Gionig is nowhere to be seen. He briefly looks for his tracks to see which way he may have gone. Sogoi knows what Pallet is looking for.

"You'll never find his tracks… breeds like him travel by their own means. They're not like us. We leave tracks. We can't hide. Queer birds, those piaminigmag. They say we keep them close by. Hard to explain why we do. Maybe belief is enough for them."

* * * * *

Gionig is now far away, closely approaching a mountain. It's sparsely covered with only a few trees. He is uncomfortable, but he doesn't plan on spending much time there. He'll be quickly in and out. This is not something he is looking forward to, but he has some obligations to Pallet. After all, Pallet got him off the island.

Looking up at the sky, Gionig sees smoke coming from the mountaintop. He lands near the edge of a clearing and walks toward a camp. He yells "Goee." Gionig hears a grunt in reply; he knows who it is. This is how piaminigmag sometimes acknowledge each other. He sees a crouched figure near the campfire. His clothes are made from black bear furs. An ominous figure, for sure. Despite his kickass appearance, Gionig is accustomed to these characters.

After going through ritual exchanges, they nod to each other to acknowledge that Malsem's spell has been broken and no one got hurt. Gionig is first to make a request.

"My friend is in need of your assistance. He is looking for information about his people. His name is Pallet."

Malsem speaks like he couldn't care less. "Pallet. Where did he get his name? Pallet, Pallet, Pallet. Does he dance?"

Malsem laughs at his own joke. "Not too reliable is he?"

Gionig, somewhat apprehensive, says, "I don't know. All I know is he wanders quite a bit. A traveller, I guess."

As if giving commands, Malsem replies, "You may know I don't bother much with mortals or do you think I have an ass for a head? I don't think so. But I see he has a bit of noggin under his cap. He got you off the island and all, a bit of smartass. It won't happen again, not on my watch. No goddam way. I don't deserve this."

Malsem is feeling challenged. He wants to see this Pallet. Gionig tries to move the talk around so Malsem doesn't dwell on the fact that a mortal outsmarted him.

"Yeah… it was just luck I got off the island… just luck… no more… just luck… doubt it could ever happen again. So Siipit told him that you might be able to help him."

Malsem is not surprised: "How is Siipit? You know I was there when the accident happened. I told her to be careful playing with fire. I'm surprised she sent you to me."

Malsem is cautious because Siipit may be seeking some kind of revenge. He assures himself he is not afraid of her, Gionig, or the upstart Pallet.

"I'll see him. But what's in it for me. You may remember my motto…'where's the free meal for me.' I like moose butter too."

Gionig quickly asks, "What would you like?"

Malsem senses that Gionig would not refuse. "Well, for starters how about a nice little island for you and your pal. He can keep you company. You can have a good time together."

"Pretty desolate out there," Gionig replies. "Big lonesome. I'm willing to agree to the island; as for Pallet, well, that's another story. You know he has to be willing to go. Other than that, there is no other way to put him on an island."

"I'll deal with your pal. I know his ilk."

They strike an agreement. Gionig will return to the island if Malsem meets with Pallet.

As if a comeback, Gionig says, "This time leave some tracks. He may not listen to you otherwise; he won't pay any attention."

"I'll leave rabbit tracks. He's familiar with those. A really big hunter he is. Big rabbit hunter."

"Good for me. Good for me," Malsem says to himself.

CHAPTER 18

Taapoategl rolls a smooth stream-tumbled stone in her hand, cupping it and rolling it over and over. Over and over she holds it tight and then releases it. She blows warm breath into her cupped hand, as if trying to bring the stone to life. She wants to feel the life of the stone in her warm hand. But the stone lies still; it feels good to touch but it doesn't move. She picks up another stone but it's not the one she is looking for. She is looking for pebbles of a certain pattern or shape that will help her aunt's spirit in the next world. Taapoategl is not worried about taboos. She is secretly looking for a small pebble that will be the perfect gift, a pebble that looks like a bellybutton. She doesn't find exactly what she wants, but before she leaves she picks out two snow-white pebbles to include in the ceremony. She leaves the brook to look for other gifts.

She now gathers enough sticks to make a scaffold. She binds the sticks together with spruce roots. The scaffold comes up to her knees.

"It's a small one but will do just fine," she thinks.

She goes to a large spruce tree behind the cabin, slips behind the trunk, and gathers gum to include in the burial.

"Attaoisoogatiget will need gum to build her canoe and water containers, or she might enjoy some gum to chew on."

She remembers that besides ceremonial offerings, necessities are included in a Nigmag burial: stone tools, bone knifes, animal pelts, and food, which are needed to survive in the next world. She will use the gifts she has, dry grass and leaves.

Taapoategl stops to think about what she remembers. "Attaoisoogatiget will need these as offerings to her ancestral spirits.

It's good to send gifts ahead, just in case. It's better to gift than to be gifted. To gift means you're thinking ahead, taking time to think what would be a good gift. Attaoisoogatiget will be a messenger for the Nigmag and also a gift to the spirit world. We come to this world as gifts, we leave this world as gifts."

Taapoategl includes all she has gathered with Attaoissoogatiget's hair in the masgoi lesgiigen. She thinks carefully about where to bury her aunt. It has to be a safe place where she will not be disturbed. It should be a place near where her bellybutton is buried, but that is impossible because of the circumstance. She will have to do the best she can. She looks at all the trees behind the cabin and picks out a tall pine.

"This tree will be an excellent marker. I can bury auntie underneath the large roots. I can dig a hole on the far side of the tree where the gentanteget and the woman will not see what I'm doing."

After she has picked out the place by the tree for the burial, she doesn't yet clean off the area so as not to attract attention to what she is doing. She thinks about how useful a caribou antler is for digging and begins looking for a one to make the gravesite. Caribou travel though Tlaagati in search of food so it would not be unusual to find an antler. She remembers how the Nigmag used them for moving snow, digging in the garden, digging graves, and for decorating their dwellings to show their hunting prowess, but she knows such decorations often just showed the ability to collect antlers.

Taapoategl cannot find a caribou antler but keeps searching the yard for something to dig with. She stirs up a place where small plants are especially thick and uncovers a pile of bones. She clears away the leaves and moves the bones around. Most of them are small, maybe rabbit, partridge, or dog. She keeps poking and finds a bone that looks like a moose shin. She knows this will make a good tool. The Nigmag use sharpened moose shins to scrape fat and tissue from pelts so they dry properly.

She picks up the shinbone, takes it to the brook, and breaks off one end by hitting it with a large stone. This splintering makes a pointed end with sharp edges. She now has a good digging tool that she hides in the shed. She will begin digging tomorrow.

In the darkness of the backroom, she continues her otootaen, her remembrance of Attaoisoogatiget. "It cannot be… it cannot be. I saw her only this past one winter moon overhead. I was anxious to meet her at the summer gathering. I knew I shouldn't have favorites in the family, but it was Attaoisoogatiget who brought a smile to my eyes. She always had something to say, something interesting. When my mother and Attaoisoogatiget got together, it was like having two mothers. I was looking forward to eating auntie's famous moose butter. Her mixture of moose meat, fat, and bone marrow was so delicious."

Taapoategl remembers when she used to gather masgoi in the early spring with her mother and Attaoisoogatiget. Her aunt particularly enjoyed this time of the year when the days kept getting longer and longer and there were no biting flies. The women had a knack of knowing when to harvest the bark; they knew just the right time. To harvest too early meant the bark is hard to peel off, but to harvest at the right time meant the bark, with a little help, literately fell off the tree.

Taapoategl thought about how much her aunt and other Nigmag knew about reading the signs of survival, about living within the gifts of the land's natural cycle. The Nigmag knew when to harvest from several trees: the basket tree, the snowshoe tree, the sugar tree, and the canoe tree. If you needed a canoe, you had to know when the masgoi was ready. At a certain time the sugar trees would drip with sweet water. The older timers used to say the trees are so full of juice you can squeeze them for a sugary drink.

She thought of other trees like saoopogeetj [grey birch] that served other purposes. Woodpeckers would descend on the newly peeled tree and immediately start pecking holes in the trunk. Before long these holes would fill up with sap that the woodpeckers sucked up. Other birds and even insects would then come to drink the sap. The Nigmag said the birch tree is touched with a special gift because of the many resources it provided. The grey birch was touched with the circle of giving in the relationship between the Nigmag, the woodpeckers, other birds, and the insects.

Besides harvesting masgoi, Attaoisoogatiget also enjoyed gathering and preserving food, either by smoking or air-drying it. Her favourite was blueberry paste made from crushing large quantities of blueberries, then spreading the paste on a sheet of masgoi. The paste would dry and could be eaten right away or stored for winter. She particularly enjoyed her blueberry paste in mid-winter. She enjoyed her food and often said that to feel good you must eat well, and to smell good you had to be healthy. She ate only food that she and her family harvested and was always in good health. She avoided the cousins' food. Such memories of her auntie filled Taapoategl with both happiness and grief.

CHAPTER 19

Sogoi tells Pallet to see Ginapeoisgo, the piaminigmag of strength, before he looks for Malsem.

"Ginapeoisgo? I've heard of Ginapeoisgo. Suppose that makes sense."

Pallet has learned to look at both sides and understand that the Nigmag has as many female as male piaminigmag. He feels comfortable about looking for Ginapeoisgo first.

"Ginapeoisgo is related to all of them, to Glooscap, to Malsem, and who knows who else," replies Sogoi. "They're quite a bunch for sure. One misstep and sometimes that's all they need. But Ginapeoisgo is generous and it doesn't hurt to get ready by getting all the help you can."

Pallet gives Sogoi the gift of a wooden flute he has made. Her eyes light up when she sees the double curve designs Pallet has carved on it. She immediately tries to play it, but without much success. She will have to practice until she learns how to play it, but she is delighted with the gift.

When early morning comes, Pallet is ready to go. He has made all his preparations the night before. Sogoi and Pallet do not speak much. Pallet leaves the cabin and after a few paces, he stops and turns around. Sogoi points her lips towards the mountains in the north. He knows where to go. He sets out at a steady pace on a little used trail that follows a brook.

After days of steady travel, Pallet feels he is getting close. In the morning, as the shadows of night are quickly waking up and scurrying away in the sunlight, he smells smoke. Later in the day he comes to a camp. Before he enters he yells, "Goee," and stands in silence waiting to be invited to enter. He doesn't move. He has made an announcement and no one responds.

"Could be embarrassing," he thinks and again yells, "Goee."

"Eptjilaasi," comes the voice of an elderly woman speaking with authority. "Please sit near the warm stones. I heard the first time. I am busy skinning a rabbit for our supper."

"Thank you grandmother. My name is Pallet." He is disarmed by the voice; it sounds so much like his old grandmother.

"I heard you. You're such a noisy tracker. We saw your morning smoke a couple days ago."

"Thank you for your welcome. I've come to see Ginapeoisgo."

"She's away. Ought to return before morning. It's not always safe anymore to travel in the dark. People hunt in the dark now; shoot first and skin later."

"Yes, times change."

"I've learned that time has no time, but can sure do a lot."

Pallet pulls out and offers seashell beads he had received from his grandmother. She had been a maker of wampum that recorded family history and of beads to trade or to use as a gift.

"You are welcome to share our oigoôm."

"Thank you; I'm too used to sleeping in the open. If it's ok, I'll make my shelter?"

With a voice that makes a sound like only a grandmother can make, the elderly woman says, "Yes."

As night falls, Pallet makes an anapiigan at the edge of the camp. Without notice or a goee, a raven flies into the camp, barking like an old dog.

> Gaag, gaag, gaag. Getaapegiee. Gigsatoi.
> Gaag, gaag, gaag. I sing. Listen to me.

Gaag, gaag, gaag. Gigsatenn ntapegiaen.

Gaag, gaag, gaag. Listen to my song.

Gaag, gaag, gaag. Gigsatenn engamlamon.

Gaag, gaag, gaag. Listen to my heart.

Gaag, gaag, gaag. Getapegien? Gigsestasi.

Gaag, gaag, gaag. Do you sing? Listen to yourself.

Gaag, gaag, gaag. Paagoamogsin. Angamsi.

Gaag, gaag, gaag. Good to see you. See at yourself.

Gaag, gaag, gaag. Paagoamoogsi. Angonmitesg.

Gaag, gaag, gaag. I look good to see. Look at me.

"It is good to see you... Gaaotj. This is Pallet. He has come to see Ginapeoisgo."

"Good luck with that. Like most immortals, she is not very dependable. But she was just behind me. Immortals, they think they are royals and have to have forerunners to announce and secure their arrival. She may be late. She was tied up with her friend."

Pallet and Gaaotj exchange greetings and nod to each other in further acknowledgement of who they are. Gaaotj flies to his perch on a tree and looks over his domain.

As he gets his bedding ready, Pallet sees a person walking up the trail. Everyone's attention is on this person. But Pallet is most interested to see that she is walking a hand width off the ground. He doesn't know who it is, let alone *what* it is. But he recognizes the Nigmag hook and feels at ease.

The person yells, "Goee," and walks right into the camp.

Without moving, grandmother greets her with a nod. "This is Pallet. He has come to see you. We weren't expecting you until later. How's Mimiges?"

"She's fine. She still flies off the handle too easily, but otherwise is fine."

Ginapeoisgo hands grandmother a bundle covered with leather.

Grandmother looks inside and smiles. "Thank you toos."

Pallet had half expected Ginapeoisgo to coming flying in. Before she arrived, he had thought that Gaaotj was Ginapeoisgo. He was not sure what shape or form the immortals would come in. Knowing he is in the presence of greatness, Pallet respectfully walks over to Ginapeoisgo and tells her he is glad to meet her and thanks her for their hospitality.

"Môtoitamo," [Don't mention it.] is all Ginapeoisgo says.

"Oelaalin," [Thank you.] Pallet replies.

"Been travelling long?"

"It seems long from when I started, but now looking back, it doesn't. I could sum it up on a small piece of masgoi. I wouldn't need a whole tree. It has been naan [five] hard winter moons overhead that I first left my grandparents house after they passed on. Since then I have been travelling toward today. I am happy and fortunate to be here to meet you, grandmother, and Gaaotj."

"We've heard about you. I'm glad you're here. We don't get many visitors anymore."

"I didn't know I could come and visit."

"Not everyone knows. Not everyone can."

As a guest, he is allowed the first pick of a meal, but instead he first serves portions to his hostesses. He gives the hind legs to Ginapeoisgo and grandmother, the spine to the raven, and keeps the two front legs. He also gets nuts and dried berries from his bag and offers them to his guests. With satisfied stomachs and happy minds, all is well.

Pallet tells Ginapeoisgo why he has come to see her. She nods approvingly. He is looking for information and stories about the Nigmag. He is also interested in whatever heroic stories she wants to share. Feeling brave, he says that at first he was just interested in meeting her, but now that she here it is different, and he has many questions.

"Go ahead."

Pallet asks, "Why did you leave the land of the Nigmag?"

"I did not leave," Ginapeoisgo replies. "I was pushed away by new religions and new beliefs."

Ginapeoisgo is brief with her answers. This makes Pallet more alert.

"I found a map that was in a *captaine des sauvages* cave. Gionig and I went there together."

Ginapeoisgo nods and lips northward as she says, "It is an old map of Tjigon."

Pallet shows her the list of names on the bark.

Without a break in her facial expression, she says, "It's a list of the ancient Nigmag names."

Pallet is quick to respond, "Where would I find the relatives of some of these children?"

"That's four questions. You should know better than to ask more than three."

Disappointed, Pallet acknowledges he has been too eager. He then makes an offer of needles and a clay pipe to Ginapeoisgo.

He then says, "I'd like to share a story with you that I heard a long time ago. It's about the fiddlehead, the wonderful spring food."

Ginapeoisgo looks toward the grandmother. They have both heard the story before, but grandmother nods and encourages Pallet to tell his story.

He sits down next to the fire, stokes it, puts on the Labrador tea, and makes himself comfortable. He begins to tell the story about the fiddlehead.

"Well, everyone knows this story; it's a story about Glooscap and Malsem, the twins. It was an early time for the Nigmag and the connection between the shadow world and the above-ground world was practically nonexistent. The gods or representative of gods and people of the above-ground mingled freely; both seemed content to mingle and co-exist. Some people argue that it was really just one world because of the co-existence.

"Gods living with above-ground dwellers are difficult to understand. Why would someone in an ethereal position want live on the ground? The ancient Nigmag said the gods were lonesome and found good company living with people. Many argue that Glooscap and Malsem were born from an earth-born mother who was impregnated by the day-walker, the sun. But before these twins, there was the fiddlehead, the first green that grew in the spring."

Pallet now has their full attention. They are listening carefully to what he has to say. He takes a sip of his Labrador tea and continues.

"It was a warm spring morning, when the day-walker spotted an Oasoeg bent over, head tucked in, bowing downward, near a brook. The spring floods had receded and the wetland area was beginning to dry. Each morning, the day-walker shone more and more brightly on the Oasoeg. His light got stronger and stronger until one morning she was not there anymore. The walker looked for her each day, but he could not find her. Then one morning, the walker saw the first signs of birth as a small head revealed itself. The head was green like Oasoeg. The birth was slow. At night, the night-walker could hear her growing. The rustle of leaves or twigs, maybe like labour pains. By morning, a head had emerged from the ground. Shortly after, they were many more sprouts from the side of Oasoeg. People told how the day-walker had impregnated Oasoeg and it was the nightwalker that delivered.

"Every spring after that, the fiddlehead returns to feed the Nigmag, and each year the symbolic union of the day-walker, Oasoeg, and the night-walker are relived again. The fiddlehead now grows along many rivers of Oapenaagi. The fiddlehead was smart and knew how to survive. First it sent its centre head as food to the Nigmag. After that more heads came from the sides, and these, too, were harvested. When the Nigmag stomachs were full, Oasoeg would then send up the main head, which grew, matured, and helped spread other fiddleheads. Taagô"

Pallet takes another sip of Labrador tea, stokes the fire a bit, and falls silent.

CHAPTER 20

On the sixth day, Taapoategl is prepared for the full otootaen; it has to be done and today is the day. She has done everything she can and has everything ready. She eats her morning meal of dried venison, but also hides some of the food to include in the lesgiigen and to eat after the otootaen. A small morsel of venison will be enough for her after the burial.

She walks to the shed, opens the lesgiigen, and lines the inside with dry leaves and grass in which to nestle the remains. She carefully places the gifts inside: two smooth round river stones, several wintergreen leaves, a string of spruce root, a piece of spruce gum, extra masgoi, and cedar twigs.

Handling as delicately and respectfully as possible, she arranges the hair as best as she can. She remembers that when babies are born, the Nigmag consider them as gifts to be treasured, and that when a person dies, the gift is returned to the creator and must be prepared accordingly. After everything is carefully placed in the lesgiigen, she sews it tightly shut with the supple spruce roots. She puts the lesgiigen on the scaffold while she digs the burial hole.

Taapoategl takes the moose shinbone and kneels on the ground behind the big pine tree. She looks around to be cautious, making sure she is out of sight from the cabin. She starts to dig. The shinbone digs easily into the thick layer of pine needles that have collected for many hard winter moons overhead. The earth is soft but it is still a struggle for her.

She keeps digging and removes more and more soil. The hole is now up to her elbow. Her struggle is more about what she is doing than about the work of digging. She gets up, leaves the tree and begins to clean up the yard around the cabin, making enough noise so her abductors will know she is busy at her required duties.

She later sits on a log and looks eastward thinking of her ancestors, Oapenaagi, people of the land of the first light. She has heard stories of ancient ancestors travelling by canoe from the east to assist those who were about to die. She remembers the story about her uncle and his last words: "I can see the Nigmag coming; they are coming in a canoe; they are in the middle of the river; they have my dog, Otjigiitj, who died when I was six winter moons; I'm ready." And then he died. Taapoategl stares eastward but she doesn't see a canoe. She doesn't see a canoe coming. It is not her time. She is not ready yet. She still has to bury her aunt. This is her life goal for now.

She wonders how long she has been here. Has it been a month or two? She has lost all sense of time. To focus her mind, she recites a counting poem she learned from her mother. Her mother said an old man named Piampit wrote it:

Neotigatat nemeeg pemtjat.

The one-legged one I see hop by.

Taapoigatat gisi mesgoolit.

The two-legged one has a splinter.

Nesigatat pempittjaat.

The three-legged one is falling in.

Naoigatat getoo gigamit.

The four-legged one wants to growl.

Nanigoatat etogtesgmat.

The five-legged one has tripped on his feet.

Aasôgemigatat aasôgemtjaat.

The six-legged one hops across.

Elooigonigatat oaposoigatat.

The seven-legged one is rabbit footed.

Ôgmooltjinoigatat teoatjat.

The eight-legged one falls outside.

Pesgonategigatat pesigooising.

The nine-legged is easily hungry.

Neotisgaigatat talaateo pegising.

The ten-legged one, when will he arrive?

After reciting the poem, Taapoategl feels better and returns to digging, all the while keeping watch to make sure no one is watching. She digs until she cannot reach any deeper. The earth smells fresh and welcoming. She gets up, walks to the scaffold, picks up the lesgiigen and looks cautiously around before returning to the gravesite. She kneels and prays for a safe journey for Attaoisoogatiget and for a good welcome on her return to the spirit world.

Taapoategl thoughts and feelings are on edge. "It's hard to understand the spirit world, but a prayer of good intention will surely help. Maybe it will help auntie with her journey; maybe it will help me with the ceremony."

She tries to lay the lesgiigen at the bottom of the grave but has difficulty letting it go. She looks at the lesgiigen, closes her eyes and lets go. She pours a little water into the grave and offers another prayer for her aunt's safe journey to the other world. Taapaotegl fills in the grave automatically, without thinking.

She feels unsettled, but knows she had to bury Attaoisoogatiget and she has done the only thing she could think of; this is what her aunt would have wanted, to be buried in birchbark like her ancestors. She then inscribes Attaoisoogatiget's name on a birch tree near the burial site. She thinks other Nigmag might read the sign and know that she is buried here. Finally, she prays that her auntie's scalp will be found and returned to where her bellybutton is buried.

Taapoategl gathers a pile of pine needles and carefully covers over the gravesite, arranging them so there is no sign of disturbance. Like the old Nigmag, Taapoategl hides the gravesite as best as she can. Hopefully, she will not have to move it. She knows gravesites are sacred because they are the hidden portals by which we return to our origins. She has heard Nigmag say the portals to the past must be tended to. You never know when the past will visit the present, the two feed on each other; one could not exist without the other.

Taapoategl comes back to the yard and sits down. Now that she has accomplished her aunt's burial, her single-minded purpose is gone. She is overcome by the horrible weight of being a captive. She hates the feeling of being a captive; it's eating away at her spirit. She has never felt this way before and it's wearing her down. She knows this state is not healthy for her but she cannot help feeling this way. There is no balance here, her mind is running rampant, her feelings are out of control. She goes to the brook, sits down and sobs for her mother's touch. She cries out, "Gitjoo, gitjoo, gitjoo. Mesgei." She calls out to her mother and tells her she is sorry, so sorry. Her whole spirit collapses and the day goes into an empty blur.

When her strength returns and her mind begins to work again, she realizes this is the last day of otootaen, and Attaoisoogatiget is finally buried.

"I have done what I can for my aunt's remains. This was not something I had ever thought of preparing for. My life was safe and happy, my future was secure and now this."

Her thoughts go continually back to her family. She knows that people die and that death is something you have to deal with sometimes in your life.

"But now," she thinks, "dealing with death when you are young and all alone makes you grow older fast."

When evening comes, Taapoategl doesn't eat. The woman thinks this strange since Taapoategl always eats her supper. She sleeps lightly with dreams skimming the surface. She keeps waking up, aware she is dreaming. Although she is exhausted, her sleep remains restless all night with dreams continually coming to the surface.

CHAPTER 21

After his talk with Ginapeoisgo, Pallet knows he has to head north to find Malsem. Follow the lips, so to speak. He packs his bag and offers some gifts to his hosts. He checks the fastenings on his snowshoes. He doesn't want to do repairs as he travels further north. He replaces a heel strap that secures his boot to the frame.

He bids his hosts farewell, and asks them if they have any messages for the Nigmag. All they do is nod as if they are tied with single string attached to their heads. He knows enough not to comment or let it be known that he has made this observation.

Pallet travels steadily all day, resting only to snack and drink from a brook. At one stop, he finds a birch cup near the brook.

"Some other Nigmag has stopped here and left this cup."

He sits on a fallen log and looks around. It's clear that many travelers have stopped here. The area near the brook is well tramped down. He smiles when he sees a child's footprints near the water.

"Probably stretching their legs after they had been carried on someone's shoulders or on a sled."

He sees some birch trees with markings on them but thinks it's just a kind of scribbling. Travelling alone, there is no urgency to make camp before dark. He knows instinctively when to stop.

Pallet travels for several days until he comes to spruce covered mountains where he makes camp. In the morning, he smells smoke coming from nearby. He is not surprised that there are no tracks other than the ones he left behind. He yells, "Goee," but there is no answer. Again he yells, and this time a tall man covered in black bear skin comes out of a rock, and yells, "Goee." Pallet's mind is suddenly racing. Where's the entrance? Like he was about to hear the word of the creator, he doesn't assume anything. He introduces himself. The man says his name is Malsem and that he has heard of Pallet; Pallet replies that he, likewise, has heard of Malsem. He offers him some nuts and chewberries. Malsem says he likes the taste of summer and thanks Pallet for the gift.

Malsem speaks next, "Well, we both have the same acquaintance, Gionig, the slippery otter."

"Yes, Gionig. He likes rabbit. I haven't seen him lately."

Pallet doesn't know if Gionig and Malsem have been talking, so he has to be careful. He is not sure why, but he remembers his mother telling him, "You can hide your feelings, but your friends can't."

Malsem resumes, "I saw him a few days past. He looked a little worried. He said he was going to the island, and that I should talk to you."

"That we should talk?"

"He didn't say about what, just that we should talk. Please come into my oigoôm and have an early day meal. I've been cooking all morning."

Malsem points toward the rock. He smiles. He knows all Pallet sees is a rock.

Pallet proceeds toward the rock. It could be an optical illusion. Malsem reaches for the rock and pulls a door flap away.

"Please come into my oigoôm. Don't be afraid."

Pallet doesn't know what to do. He lifts his eyebrows to indicate uncertainty. He sees an entrance that was not there moments ago. He walks towards the entrance and, just in case it is a real rock, extends his hand to guide himself.

Malsem, seeing his hesitation, takes him by the hand and guides him in. Pallet is astounded at what he sees, a great buffet of food – moose, partridge, trout, salmon, and cranberries. He hides his surprise at seeing so much food. He doesn't want to interpret this display of food as aggression. He doesn't want to question his host's generosity.

They both eat in silence, nodding when they catch each other's eye. Pallet notices that Malsem has a peculiar habit of loud humming, almost growling, while he eats. It reminds him of a dog growling when its food is threatened. He keeps the observation to himself. He wonders how to approach Malsem about why is he is here. He can't read the dark figure, but he seems hospitable.

Pallet begins by guessing, "So, you and Gionig recently met. Last time I saw him he said you two had a disagreement."

Malsem hides his annoyance and thinks to himself, "Gionig, Gionig. Obsidian edge, sharp; like a two piece puzzle."

Then Malsem speaks quickly, almost like he was forcing himself to talk. "Oh, we ironed out our disagreement. He said you wanted to talk to me. He didn't say why."

Pallet looks around Maslem's dwelling but doesn't see anything familiar; for some reason he thought he'd see some kind of horde, but he's not sure what of. Now is his chance to tell Malsem about why he is travelling and what he is looking for, so he starts right in.

"Well, when my grandmother died, she told me I was Nigmag and she then said to find out who I am. So I'm interested in whatever Nigmag stories you have to share. I'm not exactly sure what I'm looking for. I'm just gathering information about the Nigmag."

"OK, you can add this one to your stories," Malsem replied. "I didn't kill my mother. Stories you may have heard say otherwise, but I did not kill her. There were complications after she gave birth to Glooscap."

He pauses and then continues, "Yes I remember some stories. I have to tell you there are some weird ones out there. Some I would not bother with, but there a few you might find interesting."

Pallet, mindful of what he can ask and how many questions he can ask, decides to keep it simple.

"Is Glooscap your brother?"

There is no break in Malsem expression. With a stone face he answers, "Yes."

Pallet is hopeful with that answer. He remains focused on what he wants to ask. He knows the answers are going to be short, so he has to be careful. He has prepared his questions, but they are not coming out like he wants them to. He wants to get as much information as he can. He's already managed to get information about Gionig. Pallet doesn't want to slip up and lose a good question.

"Where do the Nigmag come from?"

"From the oisgô [black ash tree]."

"From the ash tree?" Pallet keeps his question to himself.

"Are there any Nigmag bellybuttons buried in Europe?" Pallet surprises himself. He thinks he just wasted a question.

Without revealing his rising emotion, Malsem says, "Yes."

Pallet is aware he is only allowed three questions. He thanks Malsem for his help. He is stuck in a momentary silence. He has learned so much and there is so much to know. He knows Malsem will want something in return. Pallet is ready.

Malsem asks if Pallet wants to visit Gionig. If so, he can bring Pallet to the island where Gionig is.

"He's happy there and can stay as long as he wants. And to keep him safe I check in on him. So if you want to see him, you can stay with him as long as you like, and I can check on you once in awhile as well. Plus, I want to make sure you don't drown in the lake."

Pallet agrees, but wants Malsem to come to the island before the hard winter moon overhead is done. Malsem agrees. In agreements like this, you have to do what you agree to. The consequences of not keeping an agreement are unheard of; such a situation never arises.

For no apparent reason, Malsem then states, "Contrary to what you may have heard, I am not a preacher, I am not a teacher, I am just the creator's creature."

Pallet doesn't have a reply, but to show he feels no distrust, he recites a poem he had written before he started on his quest. Pallet isn't sure what to share but he has to share something. All he can think of is his poem.

Taantet

Taantet, taantet oetaapegsi?
Where, where are you from?
Getoo, getoo oetaapegsi.
I want to, I want to belong.

Taantet, taantet oetaapegsi?
Where, where are you from?
Mootet, mootet oetaapegsi.
Not here, not here I belong.

Taantet, taantet oetaapegsi?
Where, where are you from?
Gnegtjitj, gnegtjitj oetaapegsi.
Further, further I belong.

Taantet, taantet oetaapegsi?
Where, where are you from?
Gnaatjitj, gnaatjitj oetaapegsi.
Little lice, little lice I belong.

Taantet, taantet oetaapegsi?
Where, where do you belong?
Sepootjitj, sepptjitj oetaapegsi.
Little river, little river I belong.

Taantet, taantet oetaapegsi?
Where, where do you belong?
Gmootjitj, gmootjitj oetaapegsi.
Little stick, little stick I belong.

Taantet, taantet oetaapegsi?
Where, where do you belong?
Oosigôg, oosigôg oetaapegsi.
Black ash, black ash I belong.

Taantet, taantet oetaapegsi?
Where, where do you belong?
Pitoa, pitoa oetaapegsi.
Up river, up river I belong.

Taanet, taantet oetaapegsi?
Where, where do you belong?
Sitamog, sitamog oetaapegsi.
Shoreline, shoreline I belong.

Taantet, taantet oetaapegsi?
Where, where do you belong?
Masgoi, masgoi oetaapegsi.
Birchbark, birchbark I belong.

Taantet, taantet oetaapegsi?
Where, where do you belong?
Niipogtog, niigogtog oetaapegsi
In the woods, in the woods I belong.

Taantet, taantet oetaapegsi?
Where, where do you belong?
Mesigesg, mesigesg oetaapegsi.
In the sky, in the sky I belong.

Taantet, taantet oetaapegsi?
Where, where do you belong?
Gnteetj, gnteetj oetaapegsi.
In the stone, in the stone I belong.

Taantet, taantet oetaapegsi?
Where, where do you belong?
Nigmag, nigmag oetaapegsi.
Nigmag, Nigmag I belong.

Taantet, taantet oetaapegsi?
Where, where do you belong?
Sgiitjin, Sgiitjin oetaapegsi Sgiitjin, Sgiitjin.
Sgiitjin, Sgiitjin I belong. Sgiitjin, Sgiitjin.

* * * * *

The trip to the island is fast, almost invisible. Pallet doesn't remember much; he was there, then he is here.

As soon as Pallet arrives on the island, he begins making a large ash splint basket. It's odd to find ash on this island because there are no streams. Ash trees like to grow where there are streams. But he finds a good tree to work with. It has one foot on land and the other in the water, and both hands touching the open sky. There is a small vein of water bubbling up from the ground. This is where the ash loves to grow.

As soon as the basket is completed, Pallet begins to fill it with maple sap, birchbark, venison, berries, pelts, dried fish, and anything else he can think of. He makes small canoes and puts them in the lake. Maybe someone down stream in the river that flows out of the lake will find them. He keeps his pack ready to leave the island.

Most evenings, Pallet spends his time trying to piece together what has happened to Gionig. "Did he run away? Maybe this is one of those times to wait; yes, it is a time to wait, wait for Gionig or Malsem."

The hard winter moon overhead is coming to an end. Pallet feels Malsem will be coming soon. He prepares for the visit. True to his word, Malsem comes early. Pallet is ready. Before the evening meal, Pallet shows him the basket full of provisions he has made him. Malsem doesn't reveal his emotion, but he cannot resist moving his lips. When Pallet sees his lips move, he knows he will accept his gift.

Malsem is happy with the gift and Pallet is happy that he is here. There were no stories shared that night, but both are in anticipation of tomorrow. Pallet knows Malsem will be long gone before daylight, and he knows he won't be able to stay up all night watching to see what happens. So, while Malsem sleeps, Pallet ties one end of a leather string to his own leg and the other end to Malsem's moccasin. The string is just in case Malsem has other plans.

Without a sound, Pallet crawls into the basket and falls asleep. Sure enough, before the first light of day, Pallet is flying through the air in the basket. He peeks out and sees faint daylight. He unties the leather string, and then begins to see more daylight. He peeks out of the basket again and sees a large lake in the distance. He hides again and tries to figure out when to jump out of the basket to land in the lake.

Malsem is travelling fast, so there is not much time to think. Pallet cuts a hole in the bottom of the basket big enough for him to fit through. He picks up his bag, which is full of provisions. He has been gathering food while on the island. He peeks out again and sees the lake getting closer. He sees an opening in the ice on the south side where the sun shines all day and where a brook flows into the lake keeping the ice open. It is not a big opening, but it is an opening.

There is no more time to think. Pallet drops out of the basket yelling, "Dudley, dudley, dudley," all the way down.

CHAPTER 22

When Taapoategl wakes up in the dark of the morning, she feels nowhere. She is neither hungry nor thirsty. She withdraws further into the backroom. The dark and damp are familiar to her; it seems the only constant in her life.

The woman motions to her to go outside. Their only means of communication is through motions and gestures, which by now Taapoategl well understands. They cannot speak to each other. There is nothing she has to say to the woman. She lives for the moment when she returns to her family. The woman doesn't want her to be sickly, so she makes sure Taapoategl spends much of her time outside.

Taapoategl has diverted her thoughts away from her mourning when suddenly she remembers the four other scalps in the shed. She looks upward and quietly says to the sky, "They must be Nigmag scalps too, and I am their relative. They should be buried as well."

She looks all around to see where she can bury her relatives.

"Four relatives is a lot to bury at once. I have to find a way to bury them without getting found out."

There will be so much to prepare that she almost gives up the idea, but she is Nigmag and must help her relatives. Even though she feels much less obligation than she did for her aunt, she wants to help; but she doesn't know where to begin. She has nothing to offer, but then remembers her father saying that you didn't need anything to be generous. Generosity is not a thing.

Taapoategl goes to the brook and begins by looking for smooth river stones. There is a place at the base of a large rock where pebbles collect and get rolled over and over by the falling water. This is the place to begin her task. The right kind of stones will be easy to find and she can hide them until she is ready for the burial. She is now busy with her new plans and is not thinking so much about her aunt. She is glad to be busy; this is how she grew up. She was taught, like all Nigmag, to always look about for ways to be helpful. There is always something to do.

Taapoategl begins her preparations by gathering river stones. She will need more spruce root, birchbark, spruce gum, and berries if she can find them. Putting her mind to these multiple burials gives her a mission and makes memories of her aunt easier to bear. She knows that her aunt's name should not be spoken until the mourning period is done, which is when people are again comfortable to talk about the dead. This is the old Nigmag way. So for now, she gives her aunt the name "arrowhead maker" after her great grandmother.

She dismantles her auntie's scaffold and releases the sticks into the brook. She offers a prayer of thanks and watches the sticks as they quickly disappear beyond her sight. She wishes she could be a stick and float away to Tjigon, her home. She wants to be with her family.

In the evening, all the gentanteget come back to the cabin. She is in the backroom before they arrive. It is rare for them to all be at the cabin at the same time; some usually disappear for days while others stay back, or they are all gone for a quarter of a moon or more. She did not know where they went or what they did. She didn't understand what they talked about.

This evening they are very agitated about something. As the evening progresses, they begin to talk angrily, shouting and arguing, yelling over each other. Suddenly, there is a loud banging. She doesn't understand what is happening, but it sounds like something is going wrong. A fear creeps into her heart. She is certain they are talking about her. Maybe they found her aunt's gravesite.

All at once there is a huge bang, as if a tree fell on the cabin, then momentary silence. She hears the woman speaking. Her tone is harsh, a scolding tone. Then everything is quiet. After a while everyone seems to have fallen asleep. Taapoategl sleeps uneasily, waking at the slightest sound, even just the wind blowing through the treetops. She knows something is in the air. She feels something is going to happen to her. She is too young to understand her situation and there is no one to guide her.

The gentanteget are up early in the morning; they are noisier than usual. The woman brings Taapoategl food but keeps her in the backroom. She hears the hunters go outside; it sounds like they are going towards the shed. They start to argue, and are again shouting. She hears deep grunts and a sound like someone falling to the ground; the shouting stops. She now hears the woman in the cabin and a gentanteget moving around outside. She stays in the backroom all day.

For two days, she stays locked up. The gentanteget come in each evening and continue arguing. On the third day, the woman lets Taapoategl out of the cabin. She immediately looks towards the pine tree and is relieved to see Attaoisoogatiget's gravesite has not been discovered. She sits on the south facing porch step trying to understand what is happening. The sun is warm and comforting. She knows she should get as much sun as possible to make up for spending so much time in that dark hole.

Later, as she walks around the cabin, she sees four strange looking animal pelts tied to circular wooden frames and set out to dry in the sun. She stares at them for a moment and then runs to the shed. The scalps are gone! She runs trembling to the brook and plunges her face and hands in the water. She wonders if the scalps are part of the cousin's religious practice. She stays near the brook all day. She writes a message on birchbark and puts it in the brook. Hopefully, her family will find the message. Later, the woman brings her in early before the gentanteget arrive.

Back in her prison, she finds comfort in memories of her family. She remembers a story from when she was born. Her mother said they first called her mitjooatjiitj, or little life. She was such a happy baby; her bright shining eyes lit up the oigoôm. It was not long before they called her Taapoategl, two together shining lights.

She remembers the feeling of being close to her family. She had a special connection with the elders. She was always there to help them. She did many things to make them comfortable. And all the while she was learning from them, learning the language and the ancient ways. The elders were more than willing to share their knowledge with the helpful young girl. With all this attention from her family and the elders, she was quick to learn and was always ready to help the community. She touches the earth floor and makes a promise that when she gets back to her family she will be even more helpful with the elders.

Like other Nigmag children, Taapoategl had always been provided with all the necessities of life. She was never hungry or bored. Some people said she got too much attention, that her life was too comfortable. Other people saw she was a special child and visited the family just to see her. They marveled at her vocabulary. She did not speak like a child, but used words that were hardly ever spoken, ancient words she had learned from the elders.

Some people spoke enviously of her. They said she walked a "three snowshoe trail," the kind of trail made by two people who walk ahead to break a new trail in the snow. Taapoategl remembers how you can even run on such a trail and how snowshoe runners would tie a fir bough at the rear end of their snowshoes so the front end would stay high enough to not get caught in the snow.

Before she was ten winter moons, Taapoategl wanted to be one of the trail breakers but she was told, "No," and that her time would come. But she was not one of those who waited for the trail to be broken. Some people would say, "She is not one to look for a free meal." Nothing was free in the Nigmag world; everything required participation. Everyone required resources to survive. The Nigmag world was a circle of participation within the cycle of earth's gifts.

CHAPTER 23

Pallet's fall from the basket was a short distance, but it seemed to take forever. Pallet knows to hold his feet together for landing. He doesn't want to land spread-eagle fashion and become a dead river angel.

He doesn't realize he will be landing in a very shallow part of the lake. He crouches to absorb the fall with his face between his legs. He slices through the surface of the water, spreading millions of bubbles, and lands with a jolt and a bounce on the muddy layer on the bottom. His face goes right into the mud. He comes up spitting mud. He bobs on the surface, wiping his face and spitting out as much mud as he can and inadvertently swallowing the rest.

"A face and mouth full of mud is not the way to start the day, not the breakfast of the Nigmag," he says to himself as rinses his mouth and spits out the water.

He quickly checks to see if he is injured but feels no damage.

"That's a relief," he thinks.

He slowly dog paddles toward the shore, still feeling for injury. No pain in his body or limbs; all good signs. Pallet thinks Miigemooesso must be taking caring him.

He drags himself out on the bank. The water drips from his sleeves and pant legs. The mud has washed off and he feels refreshed.

"It's time for a new beginning; I have managed to escape from the island by using my wits. I have outwitted Malsem again, the gesgemataget [short cutting trickster]. Who's the trickster now?"

He thinks of his parents and grandparents; "They would be proud of me. I have been able to survive by my wits like my ancestors of many centuries."

It makes him feel good that he has inherited their wits and survival skills. He quickly makes a fire and an anapiigan. He rings out his clothes and hangs them near the fire to dry. They look like the skin of a rabbit. He unpacks the contents of his travelling bag and lays it all out to dry. He stays close to the fire to keep his naked body warm. When night comes, it seems darker than usual. Pallet feels he has accomplished something important today; he has an after-battle feeling of quietness. He looks across the quiet lake and wonders what has happened.

In the morning, he clears off the ashes and gathers together the faint embers of his fire. He covers them with dry spruce boughs and places a few larger pieces on top. He gets down on one knee, braces himself with one arm, and leans in close. With a full breath blown directly on the embers, the fire springs to life and is soon burning strongly. He steps away from the campsite to find more firewood.

"Get the good ones."

Pallet drops his armload of wood in reaction to the surprising command. His first thought is of Gionig. "Has he come back?"

Pallet yells, "Goee."

"Goee to you. Now get the good ones. You know what they are, Nigmag; the smoky ones."

Pallet turns around but sees no one. Then, half guessing, he says, "Where are you, Miigemooesso?"

"I'm here, Nigmag. Now make some smoke."

Pallet grabs some dry wood, some damp wood, and green spruce boughs, which he puts on the fire. Soon, a smoky fire is burning strongly, stinging his eyes. He moves away to clear his vision and then sees Miigemooesso floating on top of the fire. She is using her hands to cover herself with smoke. Her eyes are closed and she is mumbling something.

"Maybe she's praying," Pallet thinks to himself.

"Well now Nigmag, what's the occasion?

"Ah... going to the gathering. Good to see you."

Smoke wafts across Pallet's face. He blinks one eye and then the other to clear his vision. "I hope she doesn't think I'm winking at her."

"Do you want to come with me?" he asks.

Miigemooesso perks up and looks straight at Pallet. She reaches into her pocket and hands something to him enclosed in a fist.

"Don't worry," she says, "It won't burn for now. Just put it in the welcome fire at the gathering. That will be enough for me. And don't look at it. I have to have some secrets."

Pallet takes it without looking and puts it in his leather bag. He tells her he will do what she asked.

"Well Nigmag, remember, there is always Oetapegsin." [Where you belong.]

"How do I get there?"

"I don't know." And with these words, Miigemooesso disappears into the smoke.

Pallet is not surprised. He is very glad to have met and seen Miigemooesso again at the end of this strange journey.

Pallet now burns sweetgrass and sage, and thanks the creator that he has been able to escape from the island and survive the fall from the basket. He knows he should have made the offering yesterday. He burns a little more sweetgrass and offers a special prayer for Miigemooesso. She must be keeping track of him and guiding his good fortune.

He now feels ready to start out for the Nigmag gathering. He offers prayers for a safe journey. He knows the gathering will be on the south shore. He'll set his bearings due south. When he finds a river flowing south that will even be better. He knows there is a large river that flows all the way to the ocean, which is where the gathering will be. He will follow the river. The river knows where it's going.

Before he leaves, he cleans up the area where he camped, puts out the fire, and gets packed. He doesn't eat. He'll eat along the way. He sets his bearings due south.

"It's been a long time since I have been around people. I'm not afraid. I'm ready."

As he travels along, he sees large birch trees and makes a note on masgoi where the trees are in case he or someone else needs birchbark in the future. He travels in silence. He is focused on where he is going. He is not concerned with what has happened, how he escaped off the island. He knows where he is going.

As night comes, Pallet thinks about making camp, but wants to go further. Just at dark, he sees the light of a campfire near a lake. Like a June bug, he is drawn to the firelight, a place to camp and have company. As he gets closer, he yells, "Goee," and stops to listen for a reply. There is no reply. He picks up a couple of stones and taps them together to warn people that there is someone nearby, and again yells, "Goee" This time, hears, "Eptjilitaa" [come and sit down, all of you].

"All of you? There is only me." Pallet says to himself.

Before he walks toward the camp, he finds some firewood. He wants to add some warmth to the fire. He sees the back of someone sitting next to the fire. Pallet says, "Goee," and he hears, "Goee," in return. He feels sure it is a Nigmag he has run into this time of the night.

"Welcome, all of you," says the stranger again.

Pallet wonders why there is more than him. They face each other as the fire shadows dance about their faces.

"Criminently, you made more noise than a herd of caribou during mating season."

They both break into big smiles as they recognize each other.

"I'm happy to see you," Gionig says.

"Yes, it's excellent to see you again," Pallet replies.

They both realize what good friends they have become, close enough to piss together.

"I had my doubts," Gionig says. "How did it go with Malsem? I assume that's where you went. When I met with him he was not a happy character. He knew I had left the island and was more upset that you had found a way for me to escape. But don't worry; I had a good meeting with him. At least there were no sleeping beavers flying through the air. I asked him if he could help you. He agreed, but not without asking for something in return. He's a what's-in-it-for-me type of guy. He said he would help you if I went to the island. I agreed, but I didn't say *when* I would go the island."

Pallet has a double laugh, one of happiness for seeing Gionig and one for Gionig tricking Malsem again.

"He won't be too tickled with your trick."

"I know, but the important thing is, did he help you? Was he able to give you a hand?"

"I think so. Sometimes, we don't understand the help we get. But I think my experience with him helped me realize something important."

Cautiously, Gionig says, "We have to be extra careful with Malsem, the second born, from now on. He is not at all happy, not a bit. He has been tricked by a mere mortal; and twice at that."

They share the meal that Gionig had prepared. Pallet feels grateful that he is back with his old friend, together and safe. He is moved to share one of Piampit's poems. It is poem about a canoe – what else could it be about? The canoe is one that will bring you back to your bellybutton.

Pallet begins; "After Piampit's visit to Europe, he came back talking in Nigmag iambic pentameter. Although the English language was not adequate for expressing Nigmag thought, this did not stop him from writing his version of Nigmag sonnets.

Goitin, goitin tami negee gaganin?
Canoe, canoe now where do you stand?
Masoi oapeg gagamig. Geeool oelteg.
The white birch stands. It looks good.
Siigon pegising na getoo saamin.
Spring comes and wants to feed me.
Taan tet ag tet oetjooltes tet.
Where and here, I will find you here.

Entool tami eemin. Asogamli.
My boat where are you. Cross me over.
Temig sipoo? Geetjool eemen gigtoo.
Is the water deep? I know you are close by.
Epsetgonig masoi. Neemol masoi.
The birchbark is knotty. I can see birchbark.
Gooilaates epgoo. Gloosit epgoo.
I will look for spruce root. It is good gum.

Masoi monnegee agoonôing.
Birchbark it is not time to cover up.
Gelool egtan, ganeg etel tamig.
It is a good ocean and deep far out.
Egsal tasig sipoo. Gigsaatasimg.
Cherish all the river. Listen to each other.
Gineg, oetjoô gesgenaasig.
Far, near, it crosses the shortest distance of the river.

Samoantigtog na magtamoltep.
In the water, we found what you left.
Pogteo, gaatag, asseg, agtjel pootep.
Fire, eels, clams, and even a whale.

In the morning, the friends have partridge for breakfast. Pallet offers his host a gift of a small pebble he picked up from Malsem's campfire. Gionig graciously accepts the gift. The pebble has a small hole in it, so he will be able to see Malsem all the time.

"You know I can't go with you to the gathering," Gionig says with regret. He doesn't offer an explanation but simply states what has been on his mind. They stay together in camp for four days. Pallet hopes his friend will talk more about why he can't go to the gathering, but he doesn't question him. Something is in the air between them that is unspoken. It's like visiting someone who's not fully present. Although he enjoys being with Gionig, this sense of waiting makes it a difficult visit.

Pallet has learned a lot dealing with people in his travels, but mostly he learned that everyone has their own life to contend with, just like he does. He doesn't ask, but he does wonder if Gionig attends the gatherings of the immortals. It wasn't something that had come up during the course of their acquaintance.

"Sometimes the obvious things are not talked about, as if everyone knows the answer to an unasked question," Pallet thinks to himself.

Gionig does feel he should explain further but all he can offer is advice.

"When you get to the other side make sure you check the old building with the old things. You may find something there. Ginapeoisgo was helpful with her information."

Pallet thinks Gionig might have learned about the old building from Malsem. Malsem is probably the only one he has seen since he left Pallet.

He has to ask, "Where did you hear that?" It is a probing question. Pallet thinks Gionig was about to give him full information.

Somewhat surprised by the question, Gionig says, "Malsem always knows more than he lets on. Anyway, he is thinking of moving and may need me to help him. That's why I can't go with you."

Pallet is satisfied with this explanation. The friends acknowledge the parting by hooking their two index fingers in a warm grasp. In the old days, this might have been a serious finger wrestle – very dangerous. But today, it is like a warm handshake between friends. Their past has been short and both are looking toward a long future even though in this world there are not many sure things.

"I hope to see you again," Gionig says. " Next time we'll have more to reminisce about."

Pallet doesn't want to prolong the departure and simply replies, "I hope to see you again as well."

After leaving Gionig, Pallet travels against the wind. It is good going against the wind because if there are tears they will dry fast. He is not sure which way to go. He doesn't want to make a conscious decision. He will let the spit of faith decide. The spit of faith comes from playing with childhood friends. It is a way to make a decision. There were sometimes disagreements on a how a game should be played, or on what to do for the day, or on where the ball was lost in the tall grass. So when there is indecision, the spit of faith is invoked and solved the problem.

A person is chosen to do the spit. He spits on the palm of his hand, closes his eyes, and is turned around three times or more. He then stops and does the deed. He extends the palm of the spitted hand – some close their eyes just in case the spit flies back – and strikes the spit with the edge of his other hand. If the hit is just right, the spit will fly in one direction, but if the spit flies in two directions, it's a split decision and the process is repeated until the spit flies in one direction. When this happens, that is the decision; there is no argument.

So this is what Pallet does today. He holds out his left hand, leans over, and spits on the palm. He closes his eyes, turns around twice, stops momentarily, and turns around one and half more turns, opens his eyes and strikes the spit; it flies quickly from his hand and falls like a judge's gavel in an arc to the south. That's it. No questions. He is going south.

He travels at a leisurely pace, lingering here and there. He is in no hurry. Although he is still young, he feels like he has had a lifetime of experience. He wants to savour what he has experienced and what he has learned. Just as when he began his quest, he still enjoys his time alone, but now for different reasons. He has changed. He is no longer looking at everything as a religious experience, so there is no grasping for hypersensitivity to his surroundings. He has found, or is on his way to finding, what he is looking for.

As he savours this time, he is looking for signs his ancestors may have left. Maybe he'll find a living totem pole. He pays close attention to everything around him. His mind is calm, his attention clearly focused. He looks at the woodpecker holes. He wonders if this is a tree where the Nigmag left messages. Many old trees have died and fallen, but this doesn't stop him from looking. It takes a long time for a fallen birch to disappear.

As he looks at both the fallen and living birch, he wonders if anyone is still using the Nigmag code. It's a simple code, more like a graph with several coordinates; maybe people agreeing to meet; maybe hunters telling of good game or good berries. Pallet isn't looking for anything in particular, but he is alert for any signs that may be around. He closes his eyes and centres his attention on the immediate day.

Spring is coming early this year. Pallet finds some wintergreen leaves. It's good to taste fresh plant food. He has been eating mostly dried plant foods all winter. It is now the season for maple sap tea. He bores a small hole in a sugar maple tree and inserts a spout. The sap runs steadily from the hole and drips into his birchbark container. The first run is best for mild sugar maple tea. This is something his family made and he has acquired the taste.

When the bark container is full enough, Pallet puts several hot stones in the sap. He heats additional stones in his campfire and swaps cooled stones for hot stones until he has boiled the sap down to syrup. Light syrup is good for sweetening tea or he can continue to boil it down until he has maple candy. If he catches a trout, coats it with maple sap, and cooks it until a bit burned, it will have a special flavour.

Earlier in the day, Pallet made a fish weir. When he checks it in the late afternoon, two trout are inside the weir. He rubs his stomach with delight. He set a trap for rabbits and a snare for partridge and catches one of each the next morning. Maple sap, trout, rabbit, and partridge; he was living a sagamoa! What had he done to deserve all this?

Before he travels on, he makes markings on a birch tree; the year and month he was here, and a "Pallet was here" kind of marking. He thinks about the old Nigmag, and wonders if any are buried nearby. He hopes they are all buried where their bellybuttons are. He knows where his bellybutton is buried.

"If you know where your bellybutton is buried," he reassures himself, "you are prepared for anything in life, even surprises. Sometimes surprises can surprise themselves."

CHAPTER 24

Pallet's route now comes to a path along a river heading south. The path is well used and easy to follow. He knows this means he's coming close to human settlements. A little later, he sees a cluster of buildings across the river downstream. He knows it's a small town. It's been some time since he has been among people.

He decides to make camp some distance from town, he doesn't want to get too close. He wants to make a gradual adjustment, make sure he is ready. He sits by his campfire and looks toward the town. The town is busy with people, cars, lights, and noise; day noises, night noises, they never stop. He hasn't seen so many people for a long time. He hears dogs barking. Maybe they are barking at him. He feels different, but he is not afraid. In the back of his mind, he feels good.

"This is a new adventure, and I'm not alone anymore." He says quietly to himself. He needs time to decide what to do next and to assess how to act in this new situation.

In the morning, Pallet walks through the covered bridge that crosses the river. The bridge is long and rundown with boards missing. The red paint has faded to pink. Bird nests built with mud cling to the rafters. Bird droppings are everywhere. He stops half way across the bridge. He is reminded of a Nigmag long house, which he has not seen, but imagines it would be similar to the bridge but much cleaner. He jumps up and down. The bridge doesn't move. It's a solid house floating over the river.

"Something to tell about by the campfire," he reminds himself.

When he comes out of the bridge, Pallet is standing in the middle of a road, one foot on the left, one foot on the right. He momentarily looks at his right hand for guidance.

"No, this is not a spit decision."

Directly across from the bridge he sees an old building and is strangely drawn to it.

"Maybe this is the old building Gionig told me to watch for. Perhaps this is it; if not, I'll keep looking."

The building looks like an old warehouse, two stories, clapboard siding, peeling paint, with rusty nails like eyes showing through. He's glad it's on the edge of town, away from the busy section. The rusty eyes all look at Pallet, watching and waiting. Without a blink, they follow him as he walks around the building.

"Who knows what it was once used for, or is used for now? Maybe I don't want to know."

Then, suddenly he sees the faded sign, "Old Fort Museum." He is now certain he has found what he is looking for. The museum is not yet open. He waits by the steps. It's no surprise that some people passing by are curious about his appearance. He easily dispels their apprehension by being polite and friendly. He feels strange; he has not spoken English or French for a long time but they easily come back to him.

"Hello, bonjour, hi, good morning, c'est une belle journée, how r ya." He doesn't say who he is, but people seem to know. He is careful because he knows for some people "Nigmag" means a foolish person. Pallet reminds himself that people who think like this are just trying to feel good about themselves by putting others down.

By mid-morning, an older man comes to open the building. Without waiting, Pallet goes in. The first things he sees on display are a faded military uniform, boots, and a collection of someone's personal articles: a book, a knife, and a musket. A set of bagpipes is proudly displayed behind the uniform, well worn but still looking playable. He knows it too is an instrument of war. How many times did these pipes lead the battle cry?

Without further delay he walks past other exhibits. They do not much interest him, but it is his usual caution and habit to scan and scope out whatever he sees when he enters a room. He finds the caretaker and asks to see the birchbark collection. The man is taken aback; no one ever asks to see the bark collection. Hardly anyone even knows the museum has a bark collection; it has been here from way before his time. He knows that some of the bark had been used as insulation in old houses and had been donated by people who thought it should be saved. Some of the collection had come from an abandoned church and some had just been left on the museum's steps.

The caretaker leads Pallet down a hallway adorned with photographs of leaders and military people.

"How strange what people save and hang on their walls. History comes in many shapes and shades of meaning," Pallet muses.

He is led further into the building. He follows his guide upstairs into a dark room filled with items in storage.

"Here," the caretaker says, "You'll find the bark collection."

The space is full of artifacts and dust. Some dust so old and thick it has become a kind of crusted dirt. The place looks like there might be more dust than artifacts. The caretaker leaves and Pallet starts rummaging carefully through the items before him. As the dust is disturbed, it seems to protest, rising and spreading like a mist protecting the contents of the room from sight. Pallet begins to cough as dust enters his nose and throat. It is so bad he has to go outside to clear his breathing. He sits by the river to catch his breath and collect his thoughts.

"How did Gionig know about this old building with its old things? How did he know about the bark collection? If there is a bark collection here, no one has seen it for a long time."

He knows he has to go back in and face the dust, no matter what. He takes a cloth from his bag, dips it in the river, wrings it out and ties it to cover his nose and mouth.

By the time he returns, the dust has somewhat settled. He looks through some boxes and then starts going over the shelves. He finds a stack of history books, some bent and beat up from use, some have broken spines from misuse.

He returns to his work but is frustrated by the jumble of useless material he finds everywhere he looks. This feeling quickly changes, however, when he moves another stack of history books and finds three small birchbark canoes with writing on them. They are a bit rough and tattered, but the writing is still faintly visible. He carries them to a nearby window, not sure what to make of them. He can only guess who may have made them. Even though the writing is hard to read, he copies it in his notebook. Some of the writing is covered with a layer of dust and dirt that has hardened into a kind of patina on the birchbark. How old are these small canoes? Pallet knows he has found something important. He knows the writing is ancient Nigmag script, gômgoetjoigasigel. He knows it is old because he is not able to read it. He sits in silence.

As Pallet leaves the building, he stops to thank the caretaker. He is obligated to give him a gift. He takes an arrowhead wrapped in birchbark from his bag and offers it to the caretaker who receives it without much fanfare. He seems to be familiar with the Nigmag practice of gift giving.

As Pallet crosses the bridge, he studies the geometric lines of its structure. He sees an X pattern that reminds him of an hourglass. He thinks of time and what it means.

"Time is here as long as you can breathe."

He sits down on a large flat rock at the end of the bridge and begins to breathe slowly and deeply with the increasing realization that time can be slowed down with breathing.

"It's so basic; people want to keep breathing, this is what we do."

He continues sitting, breathing deeply, slowly, deliberately into a slowing of time, and then, to make sure he still can, back to a faster, normal rate.

He gets up, walks on to his campsite and enters without a "Goee." It would be odd to announce your entrance into your own campsite, yet he feels like he is coming to a new place. He isn't sure what he is finding in the Old Fort Museum but it must be important for Gionig to have sent him there. He'll have to go back.

He doesn't think to prepare a meal although there are plenty of trout in the river. He still has nuts and chewberries in his bag. But what he is looking for is not in his bag. He is still looking for something. What is he looking for?

Pallet stays near his camp the rest of the day. Even before dark, he lies down in his anapiigan. Smelling the fir bows that make his bed brings him comfort. In the morning, he burns and offers sage to the creator for strength to keep looking. He asks for strength to be ready for what more he may find at the Old Fort Museum. No dreams had come to him during the night. This is good; he is glad no dreams had come. He wouldn't know what to do with his dreams if they were a result of yesterday's activities. Sometimes he takes dreams as premonitions and spends time trying to figure out what they are pointing to. He knows dreams can be just dreams with no particular meaning; but sometimes dreams can channel energy and influence future events. He doesn't want to know the future; he wants it to be a pleasant surprise. If he knew the future, he may spend too much time preparing. What he wants is just to lead a good life and keep to a small footprint.

Pallet heads out toward the covered bridge. On the way he meets up with an older man who immediately starts talking to him. He talks about where he is from and what he has done for a living. His name is James. He has lived a long life and is now retired. He is very chatty and seems to have a lot to share. Pallet tells him who he is and where his is from, which perks James' interest.

"Yes, I have known many Nigmag. They're good workers, very industrious. They're never late for work and never leave early. But when…"

Pallet interrupts; he knows what is coming. "So how's your garden this year? Plant many tomatoes, cukes, and beans?"

"Yes, I grew up near a reservation. I know a thing or two about them. I know they're smart and religious, always going to church. Now on Saturday night, well, that's a different story."

Pallet studies the old man. This is James' chance, his cathartic opportunity. He has a captive audience. He would not miss this chance. He has a juicy bone in his mouth and he's going to chew on it for all it's worth. He is going to unleash his lifelong observations about the Nigmag on Pallet.

Again Pallet interrupts. "Do you have many kids, James? They're good to have around. They're always getting into something mischievous. How many do you have?"

"You Nigmag people are very smart. They fix a broken chair pretty quick. They're very good with their hands. I've seen them work all day at splitting firewood. They wouldn't stop until the woodpile was all split. They wouldn't take any money for their work. No sir, they wouldn't. They preferred…"

"You getting much rain this year? Rain is good for the fish and the wells. It's been dry lately. Maybe we should pray for rain."

"You know the Nigmag have been around forever. Took care of the land really good. Just used what they needed. No more than that. But you Nigmag like a celebration. A bit too much I'd say."

"So how's the new government coming along? Seems to be the same old, same old – just more of the same. At least you know what you're getting, always a ton of promises. I don't know how to tell kids it's ok to break a promise."

"You got to hold back on the celebrations. That's what I say."

"Look, you seem to have lot of issues, but I'm not your license to rant on the Nigmag. If you have issues, go see a doctor. I'm not your doctor."

"Well, those Nigmag, they think they have it all figured out. Talking about this, talking about that…"

James goes on without stopping. "I'll tell you one thing, those Nigmag are generous. Where I grew up they've been paying the taxpayers for hundreds of years. All the money that taxpayers have earned has been made possible by the Nigmag and their land. The Nigmag and their land have been paying for hundreds of years: paying for governments, elections, healthcare, law, religion, world-aid, everything. The list just keeps going with no end in sight. Everything Canada has done started through the generosity of the Nigmag people.

"Generous with their celebrations too; a bit too much, I'd say. You got to hold back a bit. I know how they are. I lived next to them for years. They think they know everything."

Pallet begins to zone out. "There's no stopping this guy."

"Regretfully... they think... I'm not... yeah, sitting there so... not your license... I've lived long enough... to rant... to know how they are... on the Nigmag... I know how they are. You put them next to me and you'll see... not your license... I can tell you a thing... not your license... or two... not your doctor, not your nurse... I have lived near them..."

Pallet knows this is going nowhere. Suddenly, on impulse, he points excitedly to the sky and says, "Look!" and quickly walks away while the old man is distracted.

"What? I don't see anything. What is it?"

Pallet walks briskly on. There is certainty in his step. He knows what he wants to do. He'll gather as much information as he can and pass it on to the elders. As he enters the covered bridge he becomes aware of its distinct resonance, a hollow sound, like the trees used in its construction are echoing their presence.

"We're still here."

He exits the bridge and walks across the road to the museum. Just like yesterday, the museum is empty except for the caretaker who is waiting for him. This morning, the caretaker introduces himself and has a gift for Pallet. He says his name is Joseph. He hands Pallet an eagle feather he found by the river this morning on his way to the museum.

"This must have been left for you," Joseph adds.

Pallet accepts the eagle feather in silence but with a big smile. He introduces himself and tells Joseph he is going to the Nigmag gathering.

Joseph explains he was not born a Nigmag, but he is a doorstep Nigmag. Whoever his parents were, they had left him at the entrance of a Nigmag home in the upper river valley region. His foster parents were Mnaetj and Niipi. Pallet doesn't recognize the names. He tells Joseph his parents' names.

Pallet hesitates, and then says, "So you were not born Nigmag. That's ok. Skin is just skin. It's what's within that tells our true story."

He is not sure if he should address Joseph in Nigmag. To save possible embarrassment, he continues to speak to him in English. He is genuinely glad to meet Joseph and tells him so.

Pallet goes directly upstairs. His eyes adjust to the dim light. He continues his search, looking for anything Nigmag, anything that will reveal parts of his history.

"Seems people with the most history here have the most difficulty finding it."

Pallet has heard that at one time much masgoi was filled with Nigmag history and everyone had access to it.

"Now I am scrounging around in this old museum hoping to find Nigmag history."

He moves a cotton tarp that is covering an open space of the floor. Dust flies up like locusts. Then he sees them; the tarp has been covering tattered sheets of birchbark. As he begins to examine the faded images and intricate Nigmag designs, he guesses they are maps. There is an odd shaped item that has been flattened like a flower in a book; maybe it was a mushroom gathering basket or a water container. It's hard to know what it was used for.

Pallet gets to the point where all he can do is stare at the masgoi. He can't believe his eyes; there is so much. He sits down and stares at the bark.

"There is so much information here."

He holds a sheet up to look at it more closely. Suddenly, it gets much heavier. He begins to tremble as he tries to keep a hold on the birchbark. Soon, he can no longer hold it up. It now has the weight of a mountain and falls to the floor. He begins to cry. He is not sure what he is crying about, but the tears roll down like heavy summer raindrops. They hurt. He breathes deeply, coughs a bit and goes back outside.

Pallet sits by the river gathering his thoughts about what he has found. He rethinks what he has to do. He has to collect as much information as he can. He can't dilly-dally about this. He keeps wondering what the writing says. It's a code he doesn't understand. He knows it's important, and he knows that lack of understanding is no reason to allow important things to die.

He returns to the museum and continues to copy the writing from the masgoi into his notebook. He works without stopping until mid-afternoon. Copying what he doesn't understand tires him out. The task of preserving what he has found will take time, but he knows there's still plenty of time to make the Sgiitjinoog gathering. He will be thorough and diligent. He wants no later doubts about having left something behind. He looks at what remains and sets aside the sheets to record tomorrow. He has a half a moon to gather everything, so there is no rush. He will be back here many more times.

Pallet returns to his camp to rest and make a good meal. In the rush of his discovery at the museum, he has not been eating as well as he should. Luckily, there is a trout in his weir.

"If I am going to be here for a half a moon," he muses, "I might as well make another fish weir. I can share my catch with Joseph or maybe others."

A feeling of deep contentment, a feeling of being in the right place, doing the right thing, comes over Pallet as he sits in camp, cleaning his trout for supper.

"I may have found what I have been looking and longing for. This is no time for spit of faith decisions. I will stay here until my work is done."

Thinking all this through, he decides to make a birchbark goiten. A goiten will make his travel down river easier and faster. He has a new mission. He will begin tomorrow. From now on, he will do the copying work in the museum in the morning and work on the goiten in the afternoon. As for tonight, he will sleep like a well-rounded, river-worn pebble.

Pallet has never built a goiten by himself, but he has been a builder's helper. He knows he can do it. It takes him several days to gather the materials he needs. He ventures deep into the woods until he finds two birch trees of the right size with a minimum of knots. They will provide enough bark for a small goiten. The surplus bark can be made into containers for trading or for gifts. He will need a supply of gift items.

He makes a small fire and burns sweetgrass as an offering to the trees and to the other materials from the forest he will be using. He is grateful he has found the birch and gives thanks to the trees for their bark. With his knife, he cuts into the bark just far enough to remove the outer layer. The tree will keep growing. This is the Nigmag way. He takes just the amount he needs for his goiten but without killing the trees. He brings the bark back to camp and then proceeds to gather cedar for the ribs, spruce roots for the binding, pitch for sealing the seams, and ash for the paddles.

It has been a long time since he helped build a goiten. He proceeds slowly, double-checking his work. When he was a builder's helper, he was hands-on on every detail. This experience now comes back to him. Detail after detail becomes clear as he starts in.

He sets up his work site near the shore where there is plenty of sand to weigh down the masgoi when fitting it to the frame of the goiten. Sitting by the riverside, he begins by making the frame. He then turns to the slow work of shaping cedar ribs and planking. The spruce roots have to be cleaned and the spruce pitch has to be melted for sealing the seams. It's tedious and sometimes almost boring work, but Pallet doesn't lose his focus.

It's not long before the town people come to see his work. He is courteous and answers all their questions. Some people come with sketchpads and draw pictures. Others make copious notes. Many people take photographs. The same people return again and again during the weeks Pallet is working on the goiten.

Finally, the goiten is ready for the water. It's the first goiten he has built on his own. A feeling of gratitude comes over him when he remembers working with his grandparents and parents. His goiten doesn't look too bad. Pallet takes time to add some decorative Nigmag designs on the birchbark. This is about more than just being practical. The adornments give the goiten a Nigmag spirit. When the goiten is launched, a number of leaks show up in the seams. Pallet heats up more spruce pitch and fixes the leaky seams. He can now travel in comfort!

With the goiten complete and his notebook full of Nigmag information, he can travel on. On the last day, he visits Joseph to thank him for his help.

Joseph says, "I may see you at the gathering."

They part with a warm handshake.

As Pallet travels down river he comes to a huge concrete barrier that blocks the flow of the water. He has to portage around it. He knows why this obstacle was built. The people who built it want to make electricity, which, they think, will bring greater prosperity. But the barrier is a killer for the river's natural life: fish, turtles, beavers, and the plants that once thrived on the fertile lowlands of the valley.

Pallet thinks about all this life that depends on the free flowing water of the river. As he paddles along, he sees dead salmon that were blocked from getting to their upstream spawning grounds. They had died trying to spawn, trying to get where they could make new life.

"What a sad death, what a waste!" Pallet muses as he feels the choking of the river.

He thinks about the many other fish that also had their home waters ruined when the barrier was built. The flow of the river slowed, the water warmed, and pollution built up. All this played a part in the die-off of river life.

He stops at several Sgiitjin communities where he is welcomed and treated well. They are called Oeligoog, "good waves." Most people know who he is. They know he had disappeared for several years, but aren't sure why, maybe a quest of some kind. Many people he meets are going to the gathering and are interested in hearing the story of his adventure. As he departs each community, he offers gifts to his hosts.

The river now carries him easily and rapidly toward the place of the gathering. As he approaches the site, he sees many tents and campers along the shoreline. He hears children playing tag and shouting out, "You're it!" It's good to hear children playing again. He steers his canoe to the back of the island where he knows the elders are gathered. He is looking forward to speaking Nigmag.

"Ah, the sweet feel of Nigmag." He can taste it in his mouth. "It's better than maple sap or sand berries."

Before he lands, Pallet yells, "Goee," asking permission to come ashore. As he is welcomed, eager hands lift his goiten off the water and place it near the entrance to the grove of large trees where the elders are meeting. The goiten is a showpiece, a symbol of who he is, of who they all are. He speaks briefly with an elder who is visiting from Esgigeoag territory. He is on his summer gathering trail and has already been here all weekend. The elder tells Pallet that since he has been gone for so long, he should go to the prayer circle and have the shaman offer a prayer for him.

CHAPTER 25

The gentanteget are up early. Taapoategl hears them moving around as they have their morning meal. They are again talking loudly. The woman brings Taapoategl her morning meal earlier than usual and before daylight she is led out of the cabin. There is finality in the way she is led out. This has not happened before. She has no idea what's going to happen.

The gentanteget are standing outside. There are three all lined up like a squad. Their eyes are pointing straight at her. She has not seen them like this before. They do not have to cover her head or hit her on the back to instill fear.

She is so fearful she can't move even though one of them hits her repeatedly on the back. He hits her so hard she falls to the ground. While she is down, he ties her wrists together. Another gentanteget tosses her over his shoulder and they all start rapidly down the trail. They maintain a fast pace, rarely stopping. To rest, they walk slower. Taapoategl's stomach hurts so much from being carried, she offers to walk.

They travel until the sun sits on the lower side of her shoulder indicating mid-day. They stop by a brook to eat and rest. She is tied to a tree near the brook where she drinks her fill, eats the food she is given, and goes behind nearby bushes to relieve herself.

Several birch trees, both white and grey, are growing nearby. Quickly, without being seen, she gathers loose bark from the white birch. With a sharp pointed stone, she punctures several holes in the outer layer of a grey birch from which sap will now flow and attract woodpeckers. They will come to feed on the sap and, of course, make more holes to increase the flow. She knows it's not just the woodpeckers that relish this sap, but other birds and many insects

179

will now nourish themselves from this tree. She remembers her life at Tjigon, and how she enjoyed watching woodpeckers make holes in trees, and how the holes – some large, some small – were often lined up in horizontal and vertical designs.

After the noon stop, the gentanteget move on without resting until late evening. Taapoategl is disappointed there is no brook at this site. A small spring provides water. She is again tethered to a tree, which she recognizes as amoôg, the white ash the Nigmag use to make snowshoes. She recalls that some Nigmag also use the bark for cleaning their teeth. She remembers being taught to make a teeth-cleaning tool by chewing on a willow branch until the end has bristles on it.

With the uncertainty about what's going happen, Taapoategl doesn't sleep well. She doesn't know where she's going or what for. But she knows not to resist because they might put a sack over her head, strike her on her back with a stick, or deny her food and water. She cringes when a gentanteget walks by with a stick in his hand. Often, one of them grabs a stick and lunges toward her just to maintain her fear.

The next morning they rise early, eat hastily, and rapidly set off on another day of almost nonstop travelling. By late in the day, they come to a cousins' settlement. The gentanteget tie Taapoategl near the door of a large building that is fenced to keep strange animals inside. She doesn't recognize them; such a different looking moose and big birds that are not afraid of humans. She is brought food and water. She eats and waits by the door. Other people arrive, look at her, and go to the house. Some do not stay long while others remain longer. They stare out the window at her. She's apprehensive. She's not sure what is happening.

After two days of this coming and going, the gentanteget rise early, untie Taapoategl, and head back to their cabin. They stop in the same places they had stopped before. Taapoategl is anxious to see if the woodpeckers have started to make holes in the punctured birchbark tree. Sure enough, there are several new holes, not many, but enough to know a woodpecker has found the tree. She is glad there is a response to the message she left on the tree. Although it was a simple message, only several holes, she is happy for the response. Someone is listening. There is hope for her. She should not give up.

That night, when they arrive at the gentanteget's cabin, she thinks back over recent events. "Why did they travel so far? Why did they take her to that new place and then come back? What's going on?" She can't find answers to any of these questions. But she did learn something; as they moved, she kept a close eye on the sun. Her father had told her how to know which direction you are travelling by keeping the sun on your shoulder. She knew they had travelled in an easterly direction. She also knew the ocean is in the east. She has relatives that live by the ocean. She so hopes someone will find out where she is and rescue her.

She thinks about the woodpeckers and remembers her mother's story about two lovers, Gôptjaaoetj and Stôgon, who were not allowed to stand together, or marry, because they had not consulted a missionary beforehand. Taapoategl closes her eyes and, with longing, remembers the whole story in her mother's voice.

"Gôptjaaoetj and Stôgon were aloitjaoet [courting]. The Sagamao and community leader, Pigsaat, supported the missionary's verdict. He further declared they could not even be together.

"Pigsaat was short stout man. He enjoyed exercising power over others. He was not someone who left the eating area hungry. He always wore a cap to cover his receding hairline.

"Pigsaat was a blood relative to Gôptjaaoetj but had a strained relationship with him. He felt his family members had to marry within a certain family boundary. Stôgon was not within that boundary. Even though the bloodlines were thin, it was unheard of for Pigsaat's family to marry within Stôgon's family. It was thought that you should marry within your own line so the family would keep getting stronger. But stronger now often meant wealth, not health.

"Pigsaat often mentioned weak blood in reference to Stôgon. So it was not surprising that the sly Sagamoa readily agreed with the missionary. Pigsaat, the bald-headed chief, seized the opportunity to degrade Stôgon.

"His first and only words to her were cutting. 'Who do you think you are?'

"The Sagamoa was a shrewd leader and an opportunist. This was a time when the colonial government paid European men to marry Nigmag women. For a fee, Pigsaat arranged some of these marriages. He was particularly apt at arranging marriages with Nigmag widows. The Sagamoa's activities were not openly discussed, and under the guise of community leadership he gained wealth from these marriages. He was known to say that he was taking care of the women folk in the community.

"Pigsaat also offered protection to the elders. He would protect their trap lines or their gardens. He made sure no one would bother them. Occasionally, he collected a rabbit for the protection service. Pigsaat was the kind of man who would not have a difficult time finding a job in hell.

"The lovers knew to avoid each other because the community was watching them. The combined influence of the Sagamoa and the missionaries was very strong. Open defiance by the lovers would have to contend with blind loyalty and unbending belief. The lovers realized they had to get away from the power and control of Pigsaat and the missionaries. They began to make preparations, but could only meet briefly at odd moments with never enough time to make proper plans. They had not agreed on a time to leave, so they decided to communicate by grey birch. Stôgon and Gôptjaaoetj were both well versed in giminigmagoigasigel. To avoid detection, the lovers agreed to write in code. The secrecy of their code would be hidden within the woodpeckers search for food.

"To avoid prying eyes, they picked out a grey birch tree that was accessible but not in the open. They agreed to leave their messages on the belly side of the tree, which faced north, away from the path where Nigmag may travel. At different times, they each took a turn drilling holes in the grey birch to get the sap flowing and invite the woodpeckers to feed and make more holes. They were certain the birds would not be long in coming, and they were right.

"The only difficulty the lovers might run into is that the woodpecker would not make enough holes for the whole grid system. The accuracy of the grid, or as some called it, 'the woodpecker calendar,' depended on the woodpecker making the new holes in regular vertical and horizontal order. Random holes could play havoc with the system. But this was not usually a problem. Once the grid was established, a woodpecker tends to come back to it again and again. Sometimes it enlarges the existing holes to renew the sap flow."

"Taapoategl is now far away in the memory of her mother's story. She recalls the details her mother included in this story and realizes what she has learned from hearing it over and over.

"For the Nigmag, a year consists of thirteen months. When deciding where to start the grid, you have to be aware of the number of combinations and the space available on the tree so you won't run out of holes. The coder establishes a row of thirteen holes to represent the months in a year, sometimes called the 'woodpecker feather.' To mark the time when the message was left, the Nigmag would mark on the top or northern coordinates of the feather, and to establish the next meeting or gathering, they would mark on the lower or southern coordinates of the feather. The code could be inconspicuous with just two marks on the bark. Some Nigmag would use spruce gum to plug the indicator hole at the beginning of the woodpecker calendar and the hole at the day of the meeting.

"To indicate a closer meeting time, the Nigmag would mark the top part of the hole to indicate a morning meeting, the middle part for an afternoon meeting, and the lower part of the hole to indicate an evening meeting.

"Most of time, the ancient Nigmag would inscribe their oison [name] on the bark to let others know they were there. This is what Stôgon and Gôptjaaoetj did. The lovers may not have understood the full complexity of the ancient Nigmag code, but they knew it well enough to get their messages across. The strength of their love and their determination to escape made them especially resourceful.

"The lovers left a code that was a circle with lines on either side. On the right was a larger circle with a line on the top connecting the two circles; this was their agreement about when to meet to make their getaway. The code also had three other marks. To begin the calendar, one hole was plugged with spruce gum. Horizontally, the sixth hole was plugged. The seventh hole, three rows down was plugged as well. Reading the code, one could see their meeting time: the sixth circle or sixth moon, third week, and first day of the week, the day of the new moon. This was also the longest day of the year and the Nigmag would be having a great celebration at the time. The lovers had picked their time well.

"Stôgon and Gôptjaaoetj prepared food for travel; they made enough to offer as gifts as they travelled. Gôptjaaoetj made stone tools that he could offer as gifts. He made a goiten for travelling by water. The goiten was crucial to the lovers' plan. To avoid suspicion, he hid the canoe. Like the ancient Nigmag, he hid it underwater. He filled the canoe with stones, tied on fir boughs so it couldn't be seen, and sank it along the shore of the river. He would retrieve the canoe a few days before their departure and set it out to dry in a brushy place where nobody would be walking.

"All was in readiness; each of them had a hidden a cache of supplies, including clothes, tools, and other personal possessions. They were both anxious for the day of their departure on the long journey to snogsusacadie, the land of the palm tree. This was their plan; they would follow the ocean shoreline all the way to the warm land. They both had relatives along the way who would help them. Gôptjaaoetj's relatives could hide them in remote swampland if they were in danger of pursuit. His relatives had been among the first Nigmag to arrive in the warm lands and knew the swampland areas well.

"The day came. Everything Gôptjaaoetj and Stôgon had collected was secretly stashed downstream from the site of the celebrations. The canoe was well dried out and hidden nearby in tall grass away from the trail. First, Gôptjaaoetj, then a bit later, Stôgon slipped away from the ceremonies as they were getting started for the morning. They quickly launched the canoe, loaded in their provisions, and paddled swiftly away. The river, although now broad and smooth, had a generous current that helped the lovers on their way. No one was likely to notice they weren't around until evening and by that time they would be far away. Such was the result of a community leader and missionaries trying to stop the lovers from being together."

As she returns to the present, Taapoategl remembers how her dramatic mother told this story with great animation, and the memory brings comfort, even in her dark room. The story itself, however, now seems to her a sad one; the lovers are leaving their families and community. Taapoategl wants nothing more than to be reunited with her family and community. She turns on her side, curls up, and cries herself to sleep.

CHAPTER 26

In the morning, Pallet is greeted by the powwow dancers who are getting their regalia ready for some fancy footwork. He notices the costume of one dancer in particular. In addition to being covered with the usual small shiny bells and beadwork, he has a beaver pelt around his waist. Pallet strikes up a conversation.

"Maybe I'll see someone hopping the rabbit dance."

The dancer smiles; he is glad to be here. He had difficulty getting a ride and is grateful to have made it.

Pallet returns to the common area, an arbor-like setting under ancient trees. He is welcomed and told to take a seat. Everyone is waiting for the elder to bless the food. He looks at the buffet area laid out with an abundance of eggs, bacon, toast, sausage, and fruit. He was hoping for hot cereal, but no such luck. There is so much food that it looks aggressive; there is certainly enough for everyone to eat all they want. The head cook's round face and large eyes shine like the midday sun. He is beaming with pride over his contribution to the gathering.

Pallet sits down by a trader who is selling sweetgrass and various decorative trinkets.

"How's it going?" he asks.

"Pretty well," the trader replies. "For some reason the crucifixes are selling well."

"I used to sell dope," he adds in a confessional tone. "But now, I only smoke the pipe of Jesus for a supernatural religious high, as I like to call it. It gives me all the flat line I need."

The trader is free with his information. Pallet didn't pry because he didn't want to be questioned about his story. He wanted to tell his story on his own terms. He wanted to wait for the right time. He didn't want to be rushed, interrupted, or cut off in the process.

When mid-morning comes, the announcer at the microphone starts chatting up the dancers and chanters. He tells them to strap on their moccasins and tune up their powwow drums. He starts making off-colour jokes to fill in the time until the dancers are ready. An elder gets up and whispers something in his ear. The jokes disappear as quickly as moose butter at a buffet table.

Pallet walks to the elders' tent. He isn't sure about the protocol so he announces himself with "goee." Protocol can change from place to place, so it's good to be careful. He stands by the entrance waiting to be acknowledged and invited in. An elder nods him in. He looks around. One elder is sleeping; others are involved in a serious discussion. Pallet approaches the nearest grandmother, offers her some sweetgrass, and asks permission to speak to the group. She accepts the gift with a nod, and points with her lips to the front of the group. Pallet walks to where she pointed. An elder nods to him. Pallet understands he has to wait.

The tent is busy with pockets of conversation. Pallet can't help but hear what is being said. He picks up on one conversation that's especially interesting. The elders are talking to a young man who wants to donate his organs. He says he has led a good life, for which he is grateful, and is willing to share what he has to share when he passes on. He is not sure what to donate but he trusts the doctors. He is an especially altruistic person and has another request for after he dies. He wants to be scalped and have the bounty money collected. He explains that the bounty laws for Nigmag scalps are still in effect; they have never been taken off the books. So, he says, according to the law, it should still be possible to collect the bounty. The young man suggests the bounty money should go to a worthy cause like the government. The elders have heard that the bounty law has never been rescinded, but this is a confusing request. Who would do the scalping? Who would get paid? Where should the money go? What should the money be used for? These are difficult questions. Nobody can answer them.

The conversation interests Pallet. He wants to learn more, but it comes to an end and the elders nodded to him. He now has permission to speak.

Pallet introduces himself in the most polite Nigmag he knows, and tells of his past journey. The sleeping elder receives a nudge, clears his throat and sits up. Pallet tells of the masgoi he has and of the masgoi he has seen. He tells how he copied the writing code from the birchbark in the Old Fort Museum. He explains that he understands very little of it. He then takes out the masgoi he has been carrying in his travelling bag. He takes out his notebook and opens it to the pages of code. The elders gather around the bark. Some are confused but all are interested.

While Pallet is still talking, he is interrupted by one of the helpers. She asks if one of the elders can come bless the midday food before it is served. One elder volunteers and leaves the tent. A short time later, food is brought in for the elders. A small child has wandered in and is playing near the entrance. More food is brought in and offered first to the child, who, with a happy smile, sits down and begins to eat.

As Pallet is watching all this, an idea pops into his head. He has something more to say. He clears his throat in preparation, but no one gives him the nod. He clears his throat again just in case he is asked to speak, or is asked his opinion. He quietly eats a little and waits patiently. He doesn't want to overtire the elders. He asks if they want a break for now. One elder rises and tells Pallet to come back in two days. They want to review his story and look at the birchbark. Pallet nods his head and leaves.

Someone asks him if he wants to enter the sweat lodge. He thanks them for the offer and tells them he is not ready. He feels his cleansing will come when the elders have read all the masgoi. Pallet joins a circle where the storyteller is talking about lobsters. Pallet listens with interest; "Maybe I'll learn something."

"Yes siree dough boys, the fishers come with a boatload of lobsters, run up to the wharf. Seven totes full of lobster are brought in one boat and other boats come in with similar amounts. The captain usually tosses me a couple of lobsters for all the help. Sometimes the captain is not so generous but that doesn't stop me from grabbing a lobster or two for my pot. In all this frenzy they would not miss a couple of lobsters. This entire resource gathering has to be done before the buyers come to the wharf and I am pretty damn good at this operation. It's not so much being able to manage resources as it is about managing people. Without people there are no resources. One has to zero in on the source of the resource. If I miss the frenzy at the wharf, I quickly head over to the community centre. Here, the fishers bring lobsters for the elders. I get there early enough to help with the distribution and usually there are a few lobsters left over. If there are none left, then I have to be resourceful. The Smiths, a family of fishers, usually had supper at 7 so there was a chance of extra lobster there. Hopefully, it doesn't come to this but this is a last resort. The trick is to show up at the Smith's door at 6:30. Now, about Oinigit, he's one greedy fellow. He'll take the food straight from your mouth. Oinigit sits there on his fat ass eating all day long. The bastard has a tush the size of a two ton truck. Good riddance to bad rubbish, I'd say."

Pallet doesn't know why he is listening to this storyteller. "Who the hell is he? Hmmm, I guess the lesson here is to know your food and eat fast. Not one I want to learn."

The next day, Pallet is summoned back to the elders' tent. He enters at high noon and doesn't come out until suppertime.

The elders ask him about the list. Pallet tells them he found it in the *captaine de sauvages* trove and it was Malsem who told him what it was.

"He said it was a distribution list. It had the names of the people who were to share food, news, or other cultural events, but it was mostly used to distribute food. The list begins in random order. If your name came up, then you receive a share. If you were not there, the list would continue, and start over again several times until all of the food was shared. It was a historic list of the people who were living at the time."

Pallet suggests to the elders that he could share the list with the people at the gathering. Some folks might remember some of the names on the list. The elders agree. Pallet goes to the central arbor to share the list. He briefly explains what the list is and that he is able to read the names because Malsem told him what they are.

Petjitatjig:

Amasosi, Oapg Oasoeg, Melgatpat, Petelmit, Gamotjiitj, Glôetpeetoa, Stôgon, Masgôpit, Geloog Gisgoog, Pemiet, Melitoa, Giseeg, Tjisiisip, Omgoesseomei, Glôgoetj, Pelamoo, ag Nmtjitjagetj.

After the list is read, people begin to gather in groups, reciting the names they heard. Several people remember hearing some of the names before; they were the names of relatives who lived several generations ago. An elder who is present speaks up and tells them to approach the elders with this information if they know any of the names on the list. Some folks said some names would be excellent for their future family members.

Pallet stands outside the groups. He is glad some of the names are remembered. He doesn't know what it will lead to, but he's sure the elders will put all the information together to be shared.

He spends the evening listening to the chanters; some of them are young and hit the high notes with ease; some chew on muskrat root to soothe their throats. Later, he joins a group listening to a shaman offering prayers. He respects the shaman, but finds his message confusing. He feels somewhat removed from all the events going on. He is waiting to hear from the elders. What will they say? He thinks maybe they are getting ready to say "no." "It takes more time to prepare a negative decision than a positive one." Waiting provides fertile ground for speculation. If they say "no," what will happen? If they say "yes," he knows what to do. Not many people have said "no" to Pallet so far in his life. He doesn't know what to think.

CHAPTER 27

Taapoategl's life is now a routine cycle. The backroom built into the hillside where she sleeps is damp and cold, even in the summer. The large trees near the cabin cast shade over the whole area. She sometimes sits near the gravesite and thinks about her family. Her only connection to her family is now buried directly beneath her. She knows that by now the sweetgrass is starting to grow tall. She searches along the brook but finds no sweetgrass. The rocky edge of the brook is not a place where sweetgrass grows. She continues to gather as much masgoi as she can, storing some in her room and some in the shed. She wonders what will happen to her.

Another moon passes overhead before the gentanteget take Taapoategl on another trip. This time the woman comes along. As usual, they leave early but don't move as fast as before. They stop more often to rest. Taapoategl is looking forward to seeing if the woodpeckers made more holes in the grey birch.

By mid-morning of the second day, they reach the grey birch campsite by the brook and stop for a rest. Taapoategl begins to gather masgoi. She moves to the grey birch. Sure enough, the woodpeckers have been busy; there are sap holes everywhere. Quickly, with her sharp stone, she marks the month, the week, the day, and the morning on the grid. She makes her totem sign, two circles joined by a line; this comes from her name Taapoategl, "two together shining lights." While writing her code, she keeps an eye on the gentanteget and makes a show of gathering bark. The woman asks her something, but she keeps pretending to collect bark. Before they move on, she is able to leave a coded message on the grey birch: "Taapoategl is here on the fifth moon, third week, fifth day."

CHAPTER 28

At breakfast, the news spread that the elders have sent for a runner. Someone said the elders were requesting a certain type of ocean food. Another story was they were looking for certain information. The reports unsettles Pallet. Does this mean a delay? With cars these days, a "runner" should not be that long.

Pallet finds a log bench in a shady area near the welcome fire and settles into wait. He reaches into his leather bag, finds what Miigemooesso had given him, and puts it into the fire without looking. As it burns, steam-like smoke rises. Pallet has an urge to reach out to feel the steam, but a voice tells him not to do so. He relaxes and enjoys the scene of the gathering. An elder joins him on the log.

"Goee," Pallet greets him. "Would you like some tea or something to eat?"

"No tea, but I sure could use some nuts and chewberries," the elder replies.

Pallet is taken aback but quickly reaches into his bag and gives what he has to the elder, who says thank you. These are the last of his nuts and chewberries. It's time to start gathering a new supply.

"Looks like you do yoga or work out pretty regularly," Pallet says as he notices the elder looks really fit for his age – or maybe he did not age at all.

"Good living, good eats, good thoughts," the elder replies, trying to be informative.

"Sounds simple enough. Life can be simple." Pallet offers, trying to add a little wisdom to the conversation.

"'Tis and 'tisn't; they all have to come together," the elder adds. "This simplicity business is usually harder than it looks. So, how's the quest coming?"

Pallet is surprised the elder knows so much about him. How would he know about that?

"Oh, the quest. Well, I'm at a bit of a rest now. I'm still looking though."

He is now curious about this elder. The elder sits looking straight out at the field, so Pallet can't see his full face.

"My name is Pallet." He hopes the introduction will be reciprocated but the elder makes no reply.

Pallet knows better than to question the elder. They sometimes know something you don't know, and sometimes they seem to know nothing at all. He knows there has to be real respect for elders and not just talk about respect for elders.

Finally, he works up the courage to ask the elder if he had to travel a long way to get here. He is trying to find out who he is. He looks familiar but Pallet can't place him. He hasn't had a good look at his face or seen him walk. Maybe if he has a chance to see him walk he'll recognize him.

Instead of answering his question about travelling, the elder says with a teasing sound in his voice, "You don't recognize me."

"You look familiar but my brain is missing a few synapses," Pallet jokes about his memory.

The elder has had enough of his anonymity. He drops a big hint. "Nuts and chewberries. Socks and shoes. Talked kind of funny."

Pallet looks at him and slowly repeats, "Nuts and chewberries? Socks and shoes? Talked kind of funny?"

The elder says, "Your mind must be a little out of time, Aptoon."

"Tooelep! What the…"

"Yep, it's me."

"Well, shib shab! I didn't recognize you!" Pallet exclaims.

"It was getting to be on the downside of lonesome out there. So the first chance that came long, I grabbed it. With all the nuts and chewberries you left, I was able to negotiate my way out of the portal and clear of my curse. This is how I really look. See me now."

"You looked different, smaller."

"Yes, the curse comes with a shape and that's the one you saw me in. It was like fossilized fat; your normal body flows and fits into the shape of the cursed body."

"The voice too?"

"Yes, the voice too. Although I miss the eloquence I used to speak with."

"It's good to see you. I can't get over how different you look. I'm sure your story is interesting. Wow! Oh, I should add another 'Wow' for the parallel universe."

"Any luck with your quest."

"My quest? Oh yes... my quest. I gave all that I had gathered to the elders and they are now examining it. I am waiting to hear what they find out. Now it's a question of when they will be ready. They asked for a runner who has already left. So it's just wait and see; that's all I can do for now."

At this point another elder comes over and asks to speak to Pallet. They walk down to the river. He tells Pallet that some people recognize the names on the list and a runner has been sent out to find more information. Pallet says he hopes this won't take much longer. He wants to start travelling again as soon as the gathering is over.

"I want to visit where my bellybutton is buried," he explains, gazing out over the water. "I want to feel the open river breeze where the fresh water and ocean water meet. I grew up where the tides meet, where the ocean tide meets the fresh water from the brooks that flow into the river."

The elder recognizes the deep nostalgia and the great importance of what Pallet is feeling.

"You should certainly be on your way as soon as the information you have provided has been understood as best as we can understand it. Some of the masgoi you brought back is very old and it takes more than one person to understand it. Some elders understand different bits of the writings and some understand other parts. It's important for us to try to put the whole picture together. You have discovered this Nigmag history. This is your story too."

Pallet realizes the elders are not ready to leave although the gathering is winding up. They will stay on. They have important work to do; there is so much to learn and understand. He feels the weight of what he has discovered and placed before the elders. He will be patient.

Pallet returns to the log where Tooelep is waiting. After further conversation they agree to meet later on. As Pallet stands up preparing to leave, Tooelep hands him a piece of rolled-up leather. He is surprised and thanks him.

"May I ask what it is?"

"Yes, it may be something that will help you find what you are looking for."

Tooelep is not totally sure what Pallet is looking for but he wants to give him something. Pallet opens the leather and sees a rolled-up masgoi. It's too old for Pallet to decipher.

He thanks Tooelep and adds, "I'll take this to the elders for deciphering."

Later that evening, Pallet is summoned again to the elders' tent. Before they can question him, he tells them that another masgoi has come into his possession. He hands it over to the elder next to him. Immediately, the others convene around her. After a first look, one group settles down to examine the new masgoi, and another group continues to work on the old masgoi. In addition, they have Pallet's notebook, which contains the code copied from the masgoi in the Old Fort Museum. Pallet is given a choice; he is welcome to stay while the new masgoi is read if he wants to. He decides to take a break until they need him again.

At midnight, he is summoned to return. The elders have more questions for him, but this time they also begin to tell him what they have learned. There are many historic notes written on the birchbark and the elders will continue to study them. But for now they are concentrating on one aspect of the writings.

The elders ask Pallet to speak to the gathering about the people whose story he has brought with him. The people who have come to the gathering have a right to know since this is part of their history. They instruct him to make notes on birchbark as they reconstruct what they have learned. They all sit in a circle. The story is then told with Pallet rapidly making notes. Tea is brought in but they are so involved in reconstructing the story, nobody notices. Some of it is missing, but from what they have been able to piece together, they have the thread of what happened.

At the end of the session, everyone is tired and ready to sleep. But before they conclude, the head elder, Goaletgon speaks: "We're all grateful for what has happened at this gathering. We will all be going home with more knowledge of who we are. The information we now have brings enlightenment to our lives. The stories we have found bring tears for our survival. I urge you to support each other, stay strong, and tell your neighbours what we have learned today. I want to thank our Uncle Pallet for what he has been able to do. There are not many among us who spend five years looking for our history. I thank you all for your support. Tomorrow at high noon we will share what we know. Taagô."

Pallet cannot hide the smile that comes to his face when he is referred to as an "Uncle." This means a lot to him because it is a term used to address a respected person, or someone who has made a contribution to the Nigmag community.

At high noon the next day, the gathering comes to the arbor. People are talking in low tones, as if waiting for an announcement. The children are playing around the yard outside the grove, yelling and running. The drummers are playing the Nigmag national anthem. All those that can stand are standing. As the anthem ends, the lead elder, Goaletgon, rises and approaches the centre of the arbor. He briefly introduces Pallet and tells the gathering that he has something to share with the Nigmag nation.

Pallet introduces himself by telling where he is from, who his parents and grandparents were, and how long he has been travelling. Before proceeding further, he acknowledges the Sgiitjinoog, their generosity, and the gift of land from the creator that the Sgiitjinoog live on and care for. He tells them that in his five years of travelling, he was following his grandmother's advice; "You are Nigmag. Go and find out who you are."

"I've travelled to many places. I have met many people and accepted them for who they are. I encountered many events and had many experiences that were new to me and I accepted them for what they were. But the most important thing I brought with me is the writing on masgoi that tells what happened to the Nigmag. Fortunately, there are elders among us who are able to read the masgoi. The elders have read the masgoi and I will tell you what they have learned from the writings."

Pallet pauses as he feels the importance of the event; the weight of it makes him nervous. "No need to be nervous when you're telling the truth," he thinks to himself. He calms down and continues his story.

"This is the story of Taapoategl. You may have already heard stories about her. She was a young woman from Tooitenog. She lived part of her life in Tjigon. Like you, I too heard many versions of her story. The elders have read the masgoi and have pieced together some of her story. Stories of her have survived through masgoi writings, oral history, and storytellers. Some of the masgoi has been found in the Old Fort Museum, in private collections, in churches, and in other museums.

"This part of story begins one spring when her family was getting ready for maple sap gathering. She liked this time of the year. The family's supply of sweet chewberries was dwindling down. The sweetness of the maple sap would be good to have. One of

Taapoategl's chores, first thing in the morning before anyone else was up, was to fetch water for morning tea.

"One morning, while fetching water, she was taken by three hunters. After she was abducted, she was kept in a root cellar in the back of a strange dwelling, a cabin. She did not understand her captors. They did not speak to her. They gestured to her when they wanted something done. One of her captors was a woman who fed her and assigned her chores. She'd gesture to her to fetch the water or fetch the wood. During her chores, she had the chance to gather masgoi from the woodpile and later used the masgoi to make miniature goitens and to write her story.

"Taapoategl was a prolific writer and made notes each day. She wrote where she thought she was. She estimated how many days walk she was from Tjigon. She also described in detail the process she went through when she was burying her aunt's scalp and long hair. There was no one she could tell her sad experience to, so she wrote her thoughts on the masgoi. She was not sure what to do, but she managed to give her aunt's remains the required respect of a Nigmag burial. The elders have read the masgoi and have concluded that for a young girl her age, she did the right thing with her aunt's remains.

"She made miniature oigoôms and goitens and small birchbark containers that she gave to her abductors. She was eager to do this because she was writing messages on them to tell her family where she was. The abductors were taking these miniatures and trading them in the settlements they visited when they went on their trips.

"After awhile there were so many notes that she had to hide them wherever she could. She always had masgoi with her and would place them where, hopefully, other Nigmag would find them. She'd hide them near large trees and at campsites. She left them under stones, hid them in tree limbs, and burned some in hopes that the smoke would carry her message to her family and they would come and rescue her. She left masgoi at a settlement barn that had strange animals around it.

"The elders have been very moved by her masgoi writing. She wrote that she found a sheet of birchbark hidden in the wall of the backroom where she was kept. The bark had names of other Nigmag who had been held captive there. She counted a total of forty-seven names on the bark and, according to the marks they left beside their names, they were all women or young girls. She wrote her name on the masgoi.

"It was a quarter of a moon after her capture that she realized she had not been tapping her feet together whenever she got up from sitting or laying down. Her mother would always tap her feet together each time she got up. Taapoategl had adopted this habit from her mother and grandfather. Once she realized she had forgotten to tap her feet when she got up, she began to do it again. Now, each time she tapped her heels together she remembered her mother. This gave her the strength to deal with her abduction.

"At one point, after a second trip, she was taken by different captors and moved to another location. She was kept in a similar cellar. She made more notes on masgoi and left them outside her prison door. She kept as much bark with her as she could. She again made small oigoôms, goitens and containers, which she inscribed with designs and writing. The notes and miniatures would disappear from her door, so she kept making them, writing on them and leaving them outside the door. She hoped that one of her writings would reach her family or other Nigmag who would come to take her home. She became more and more lonesome for her home.

"No one knew where she was after the first abductors handed her over to other abductors. Stories have been told over the years about how she made her way back to her family. One story tells of her clinging to a floating log and travelling through wild rapids. Another story has it that a Nigmag passing through the area where she had been, found one of her notes and alerted the family. But none of these stories pan out. They all end in the middle of nowhere.

"The next time we find evidence about her is when a masgoi is found in Pitjpogeg. It appeared due to riverbank erosion but the Nigmag who found it were unable to read the masgoi. They were unfamiliar with gômgoetjoigasigel, the ancient Nigmag writing. They put the masgoi away for safekeeping and it remained out of sight for many years. At this gathering, one of the elders remembered that this masgoi had been archived and forgotten by most people. He retrieved it and gave it to me. I gave it to the elders who have pieced together more of the story.

"The Pitjpogeg is a river where a long finger of ocean slowly creeps upstream each day until it reaches tidehead. The Pitjpogeg masgoi has given the elders more of Taapoategl's story.

"Taapoategl was born in Tooitenog in the spring, on the 14th day of the new moon in 1740. Hunters captured her in the spring, on the 10th day of the new moon in 1750.

"She writes that when the gentanteget had reached a settlement, she was locked in the animal barn. During the night, strangers came and tied her up. She was moved to a huge wooden canoe and locked up for two days without food or water. Although it was dark when she was moved to the big wooden canoe, she could see a white flag with a red cross on it and some other lines she did not recognize.

"During the two days she was locked up, she continued writing and making miniature canoes that she slipped under her prison door. She still had a supply of masgoi secured in her clothes. Even if they fed her now, she was not sure she could eat.

"On the third day, the ship left land. The sailors now came to her unlocked jail night and day. During the night, as the sailors slept, Taapoategl escaped and jumped overboard with her last masgoi tied to her leg.

"Taapoategl's last words were, 'Mesgei Gitjoo. Gesalol.'" [I'm sorry, Mother. I love you.]

ABOUT THE AUTHOR

Peter J. Clair was born in Elsipogtog, New Brunswick in the Nigmag territory of Signigtog. He now lives in Tobique, NB. He has worked for much of his life at the traditional craft of ash splint basket making. He has created original product designs for a variety of uses. His baskets have been exhibited in several galleries. *Taapoategl & Pallet* is his first book.

AFTERWORD

My heart is moved by all I cannot save:
so much has been destroyed

– Adrienne Rich
Dream of a Common Language

When Peter Clair told me he had written a novel, and asked me if Chapel Street Editions might be interested in it, I immediately said, "Yes." I have known Peter since the 1980s as a maker of beautiful ash splint baskets and as a person deeply concerned about the practice and celebration of Indigenous culture. I have always regarded him as an artist, so I was not surprised by this turn to writing, or more accurately, storytelling

When Peter put the manuscript in my hands, and I saw it was two stories in one book, I was reminded of Chateaubriand's famous novel, *Atala & Rene*, published in 1801 in France. Like *Taapoategl & Pallet*, Chateaubriand's story is set in Aboriginal North America and tells the story of two individuals dealing with the cultural disruption of the European invasion. Chateaubriand spent five years in the continental heartland of North America with a French exploratory expedition. On returning to France, he wrote with great emotional force about the wilderness landscape and the Indigenous people as he both knew and imagined them.

Chateaubriand, however, was an ardent Christian and his novel is essentially an apologia for the conversion of Indigenous nations to Christian culture. He was deeply sympathetic toward Indigenous people, but he had no doubt their best interests would be served by Christianization.

Taapoategl & Pallet, on the other hand, is about the effect of this forced Christianization from an Indigenous point of view. Peter Clair has created the stories of two characters – one historical, one contemporary – to portray the disruption of his ancestral culture and the long aftermath of European colonization of the Nigmag homeland.

This story has been told before. In 2000 Daniel N. Paul published *We Were Not the Savages: A Mi'kmaq Perspective on the Collision Between European and Native North American Civilizations* (Revised edition, 2007). Telling the truth about this history is an enormously courageous undertaking, which Paul's social and cultural history exemplifies.

Imagining this truth in dramatic narrative form, and portraying the power of this truth in the life circumstances of two young people, as Peter Clair has done in *Taapoategl & Pallet*, is also a courageous undertaking. An author takes a risk with a story like this, but when it comes from the heart and speaks truth to power, readers may be moved in complex, thoughtful, and deeply stirring ways.

Such is the case with *Taapoategl & Pallet*. This is a complex book; not only does it portray the dark history of colonization and its impact on the Nigmag people, it also includes detailed descriptions of Nigmag social and material culture. It layers a rich variety of traditional stories within the main storyline of the novel. Pallet's story is frequently sprinkled with flashes of humour, irony, and cultural self-consciousness.

This combination of elements makes *Taapoategl & Pallet* a book that can be read on several levels. It may need to be read more than once in order to arrive at a fully rounded understanding of its contribution to First Nation literature and to the literature of cultural awareness in Canada.

Keith Helmuth
Chapel Street Editions
Woodstock, New Brunswick
August 2017

MI'KMAQ GLOSSARY

There are various Mi'kmaq orthographies in the Eastern Provinces of Canada. I have chosen a version based on the Pacifique Orthography. Pronunciation and spelling may differ in various Mi'kmaq communities. This is not a definitive method of spelling and pronouncing the language.

There are thirteen letters in the alphabet and a number of vowels blends. The same vowels together indicate a long sound.

a . . . . ah (sound)

e . . . . a

g . . . . g/k

i . . . . e

l . . . . l (same as English)

m . . . . m (same as English)

n . . . . n (same as English)

o . . . . oo

ô . . . . o

p . . . . p/b

s . . . . s (same as English)

t . . . . d/t

tj . . . . j

Agem . . . . snowshoe

agamôg . . . . white ash

anapiigan . . . . small shelter

apôenmoi . . . . help me

Aptoon . . . . cane

Attaoisoogoiget . . . . . one who knows how to cook

Elosgatamit . . . . one who spits

epogan . . . . walking stick

eptjilaasi . . . . you are welcome

Esipisgoitg . . . . high tides

Gaaootj . . . . raven

Gaoletgon . . . . dry branch twigs

geeoooget . . . . earthquake

gesalogig ag gipalogig . . . we love them and we fear them

gesalool . . . . I love you

gesgemasit . . . . one who takes shortcuts

Gespiag . . . . northern section of NB

gentanteget . . . . hunter

giminigmagoigasil . . . . written in Mi'kmaq code

ginap . . . . a person of great and unusual
                          powers

ginapeoisgo . . . . woman of great and unusual
                          powers

Gisoolg . . . . creator

Gitjoo . . . . mother

Glooscap . . . . a hero figure in Mi'kmaq stories

gloositeoisgo . . . . good woman

goee . . . . informal greeting

Goinig . . . . otter

goiten . . . . canoe

gômgoetjoigasigel* . . . . written in the manner of a sucker fish

Gonteetj . . . . little stone

Gôptjaoetj . . . . robin

gtjipoingn . . . . million

lapaltineoi . . . . water for washing

lesgiigen . . . . coffin

malpalaiet . . . . in modern terms, a doctor

Malsem . . . . Glooscap's brother; often a
negative figure in Mi'kmaq stories

masgoi . . . . birchbark

Matjôgteligen . . . . . . arrow head

Menagoesg . . . . St. John NB

mesgei . . . . I'm sorry

Miigemagatti . . . . . . land of the Mi'kmaq

---

* See page 117. The original Mi'kmaq pictographic script, which plays a central role in this book, is the oldest writing system in North America north of Mexico.

Miigemooesso. . . . . . . a figure in Mi'kmaq stories who may provide assistance

Mitiei Nipi . . . . poplar leaf

Miniges . . . . butterfly

mitjooatjiitj . . . . small child

Mnaetj . . . . fish

Mndoo . . . . creator

motoitamo . . . . don't mention it

maapôen . . . . stick for holding fish

Nigameoeiataig . . . . . to spread Nigmag influence through intermarriage

Nigmageoeiato . . . . . Variation of Nigameoeiataig

Nigmageoeiatotitj. . . . Variation of Nigameoeiataig

Niipi . . . . leaf

oalôspgesgsoa . . . . . . quartz

oaltesg. . . . . a bowl game

Oapenaagi. . . . . land of first light

Oasoeg . . . . flower

Oasteo . . . . snow

oelaain. . . . . thank you

Oeligoog . . . . good waves

Oetapegsin . . . . where you belong

oetjgoei . . . . I am coming

oetjgooen . . . . are you coming

oigoôm . . . . small shelter

Oingit . . . . odd shape

Oiipit . . . . tooth

oisôg . . . . black ash tree

oison . . . . name

oiteneiosamo . . . . nose horn

Oôo . . . . bowl

otootaen . . . . burial

piaminigmag . . . . someone beyond an ordinary
Mi'kmaq

Piampit . . . . someone who is present

Pigsaat . . . . one who smokes

Pitjipogeg . . . . river that extends far inland

Pogseteo . . . . fire spark

pogteoit . . . . meteor

poôin . . . . shaman

pootep . . . . whale

Potlatamootj . . . . mischievous person in Mi'kmaq
stories

saalitei . . . . a generous donation

Saasap . . . . jellyfish

samagma . . . . chief

siesipeteg . . . . place of heat

Signigtog . . . . one of Mi'kmaq districts

Siigon . . . . spring

Siipit . . . . one who yawns

sgaatagamootj . . . . . . ghost

Sgiijtin . . . . First Nations person

Sogoi . . . . aunt

Soon . . . . cranberry

Stôgon . . . . spruce

taagô . . . . an expression to indicate a story
or event is done

tegpaag . . . . a cold drink

tes ag mo tes . . . . . . time and no time

tjiensigoo . . . . tall grass, sweetgrass

Tjigon . . . . knee

tjioisis . . . . large animal

tjisiisip . . . . large bird

Tlaagati . . . . where one belongs

Toitenoog . . . . where the water flows out

Tooatjeg . . . . name of river where Taapoategl
once lived

MI'KMAQ SYMBOLS

These symbols are traditional to Mi'kmaq art and design. Like symbols in many other cultures, they concentrate a range of meanings into graphic representation.

These are symbols that would have appeared on Pallet's leather shoulder bag. He might have inscribed some of them on his canoe. Taapoategl might have put them into her masgoi communications.

The representations shown here were prepared by the author.

CPSIA information can be obtained
at www.ICGtesting.com
Printed in the USA
BVHW071048270821
615078BV00002BA/15

9 781988 299112